1-18-74

A FORGOTTEN HERITAGE

A FORGOTTEN HERITAGE

Original Folk Tales of Lowland Scotland

Edited by
HANNAH AITKEN

ROWMAN AND LITTLEFIELD
Totowa, New Jersey

First published in the United States 1973
by Rowman and Littlefield, Totowa, New Jersey

© Scottish Academic Press

Library of Congress Cataloging in Publication Data

Aitken, Hannah, comp.
    A forgotten heritage.

    Bibliography: p.
    1. Tales, Scottish. I. Title.
GR144.A345   398.2'0941   73-12441
ISBN 0-87471-430-3

Printed in Great Britain by
R. and R. Clark Ltd., Edinburgh

ACKNOWLEDGEMENTS

I would like to thank County Librarians in Ayr, Castle-Douglas, Dumfries, Kirkcudbright and Selkirk, as well as members of the staff in the Mitchell Library and the National Library of Scotland for their help in tracing early versions of the Tales; and also, very specially, Miss C. L. Dickson of the Scottish Department at the Central Library in Edinburgh whose outstanding knowledge of sources is always so readily and unassumingly available.

Dr. I. F. Grant has been generous from the beginning with counsel and encouragement; Miss Rhoda Spence's sixth sense for Lowland history as well as her library have been at my disposal; and Miss E. Boog-Watson brought understanding, patience and zeal to the task of proof reading. To all three I am exceedingly grateful, as I am to Miss M. I. Wood for the incident embodied in "The Last Act". My thanks are also due to Mrs D. M. Paulin for permission to reprint "The Miller's Tale" and "The Herd's Tale" from *The Gallovidian Annual*, and to Miss Iris Stewart for help with typing.

It would be quite out of place for me to thank Mr. David Dorward of the University of St. Andrews. "A Forgotten Heritage" is as much his as mine. The language section is his work, and the rest of the book would never have taken shape without him. He has guided the whole enterprise with scholarship, enthusiasm and tact, and my sole complaint against him is his determined refusal to allow his name to appear—as it certainly should have done—as joint editor.

CONTENTS

Note on the Illustrations

The frontispiece is "A Scottish Maid" by David Allan (by courtesy of the National Gallery of Scotland).

The line drawings are by Jurek Pütter, da. des. edin. Grafik Orzel Design Studio, St. Andrews 1972.

The drawing on the dust jacket is "The Craggy Bield" by David Allan (by courtesy of Edinburgh Public Libraries).

INTRODUCTION

"There was one before now and his name was Tòmas na h'ordaig and he was no bigger than the thumb of a stalwart man"; so begins the Dunbartonshire version of a tale once familiar from India to Spain. He was swallowed alive by a brindled bull, but in the end he won safely home, "and it was he indeed who had the queer story for them". And it is here, perhaps, that we have a glimpse of the origin of the folk-tale: primitive man, thumb-sized and mystified in a vast and threatening universe—and subduing its terrors to a story.

The universal gift of story-telling can be accepted with simple gratitude, but its manifestation in similar stories all over the world is another matter. The close resemblance of the ancient story patterns wherever they occur presents a problem which Wilhelm Grimm put in a nutshell: "How can we explain the fact of a story told in a lonely village in Hesse resembling one in India, Greece or Servia?"[1] According to one scholar, this question is beset with perplexities so entangled that only the elves themselves could unravel them. Nevertheless, generations of scholars have taken up the task.

The discovery of European folklore themes in Sanskrit literature seemed at one time to point to the Indo-European people as the earliest story-tellers. This would have provided a simple answer to Grimm's question had it not been that research went on, bringing to light new sources, emphasising the savage element in the ancient tales and leading eventually to the conception of them as primitive man's attempt to interpret the basic universal situations of life. "Given a similar state of taste and fancy," wrote Andrew Lang, "similar beliefs, similar circumstances, a similar tale might conceivably be independently evolved in regions remote from one another."[2]

Closer analysis, however, made it clear that by no means all the ancient tales had simple themes, while many of them were handled with skill and even artistry beyond the power of the primitive mind. This admission laid the whole subject open to a new approach which came from Finland at the turn of the century with the historic-geographic method of research and involved the tremendous task of collecting every possible version of every accredited tale and tracing it back to its source. The work of the Finnish School, initiated by the Krohns, father and son, with Dr. Antii Aarne, has set folklore firmly among the sciences. And should any casual reader deplore such an attitude to the "collective dreams of mankind", the fact that over ten thousand motifs[3] or variations have so far been recorded, shows how much light those dreams can throw on the development of language and on the history of human ideas.

As to the actual means whereby the tales spread over vast distances in eras when transport as we know it was virtually non-existent, one can only marvel at the range of possibilities. Some stories crossed the globe with the mass population movements, but quite apart from its migrations the ancient world seems to have been perpetually on the move. By the Bronze Age coppersmiths were itinerant. Amber merchants linked the Baltic and Greece. The Diaspora scattered the Jews far and wide. Icelandic mercenaries served at the Byzantine Court, while a soldier of the Roman Empire might be recruited in Persia and posted to Scotland or Spain. Later came the dogged hosts of pilgrims bent on inaccessible shrines; crusading armies; wandering scholars; royal messengers with their servants; traders, artisans, sailors.[4] Among those intrepid travellers there would be many eager to while away the slow miles with an exchange of stories which would take root by the wayside like seeds carried by birds. Many such seeds found fertile soil in the Western Isles of Scotland, an important communication point in the ancient trade and cultural network, and centuries later J. F. Campbell reaped their harvest "by the barrow-load".

Some of these Celtic tales drifted across the Highland line to the north-east[5] and a few (losing much of their mystery and strangeness in the brisk Lowland air) reached southern parts by way of Ireland; but on the whole the Scottish Lowlands drew their folklore from the North Sea community. By the twelfth century[6] ships from the Baltic and the Low Countries were plying regularly to the east coast ports, while Flemish and German trade settlements and a series of Royal marriages brought passengers as well as cargo. And with the ships came the tales.

"The cauldron of story," Tolkien declared, "has always been boiling and to it have been added bits, dainty and undainty." A rich mixture simmered in the Scottish cauldron. History and pre-history went into it; old feasts and famines; the doings of druids, saints, soldiers, shepherds, miners, fishermen and kings; the shape of the land, the prevailing weather, the rhythms of speech. And the "bits" from far afield, dropped in piecemeal to seethe and bubble with the local brew, soon took on its flavour.

By the mid-fifteenth century the body of Scottish folklore was established, but as time went on the tales and songs multiplied, weaving themselves into daily life and thought, and for this we owe a tribute to the story-tellers, that nameless band, many of them unconscious artists, who spread the tales by word of mouth, adapting them to local conditions and the experience of their listeners. "When I'm tired of scraping gut," says the blind fiddler in *Redgauntlet*, "I whiles make a tale serve the turn among the country bodies." The country bodies in their turn would recast it until, by degrees and over a long, long time, it became enriched in language and varied in detail, the foreign elements fully acclimatised.

Under the heading of Universal Themes, a few of these products of the common folk memory have been set apart from the home-grown legends and anecdotes, but otherwise no distinctions have been made, for the traditional stories, taken as a whole, bring an exceptional offering.

When the wee bunnock plays jink-aboot and makes off ower the knowe like a daft yell cow, a whole little pre-industrial community springs up, busy with tow-rock, law-brod, goose and shears, clue, clove, kirn and sprit-binnings. Outmoded social conditions become vivid when Tibbie Dickson, the changeling's mother, picks up her bucket and sets off for the well by way of midden, peat-stack and kail-yard. And for sheer veracity, no history book could compete with that eye-witness account of the press gang in action which introduces "Whuppity Stoorie"; "Hech-how! that dulefu' press gang! They gaed aboot the kintra like roarin' lions seekin' whom they micht devour. I mind weel when my auldest brither Sandy was a' but smoor'd in the meal ark hiding frae thae limmers. After they were gane we pu'd him oot frae amang the meal, pechin' and greetin' an' as white as ony corp'. Ma mither had to pyke the meal oot o' his mouth wi' the shank o' a horn spoon." Few sources can flash the past so spontaneously back to the present.

But the tales have more to offer: a gift of which the new Scotland stands perhaps in greater need than it knows. A change of focus—it is hard to define. Ordinary things—stone, wood, water and grass, house, fire and bread—lit suddenly by their ancient significance. The bread may appear as the enterprising "wee bunnock", as the smaller portion of barley cake chosen by the lad who valued his mother's blessing, or as the flourocks and soople scones of the harvest kirn. But never by any chance could it be the sliced loaf heedlessly bought in the supermarket.

New days bring new ways; that is inevitable, but there is no harm in remembering John Buchan's warning that a land in the turmoil of change should beware of "casting aside as provincial and antiquated the things that belong to the very core and essence of its being".[7] The traditional Lowland tales may be a very small part of the Scottish heritage, but if we do not know them it is possible that we do not quite know ourselves.

NOTES

1. Grimm, *Household Tales.*
2. M. R. Cox, *Cinderella.*
3. A "type" is a traditional tale made up of one or many "motifs" or elements which have persisted in tradition. The scholar's type index is the basis for an area with a large store of tales, while the motif-index shows similarities in tale elements all over the world.
4. For a description of ancient travellers see Kenneth Jackson, *The International Popular Tale and Early Welsh Tradition.*
5. A good example is "Mally Whuppie" of Aberdeenshire, a variant of Islay's "Maol a Chliobain". Maol means in Gaelic a devotee, literally a tonsured person (Malcolm means "follower of St. Columba"); but, the word being unfamiliar in Aberdeenshire, it was taken to be a girl's forename, a diminutive of Mary.
6. As early as 1247 a Scottish yard received a Flemish order for a crusading vessel. The result greatly impressed the Continent.
7. John Buchan, *Sir Walter Scott.*

I

THE FAIRY PEOPLE

THEY were known as "the people of peace", "the seely (happy) folk", "the good neighbours"; their hills and green dancing rings were protected from the plough and their ways treated with respect. But in spite of all propitiation they remained an unpredictable element, capable as it suited them of revenge, gratitude, kindness or spite; inspired by a tricky brand of humour; given to kidnapping mortals, for whom they substituted a wooden stock or, when a child was taken, some elderly, peevish, unattractive, thoroughly expendable (though musical) member of their own race.

"As active as squirrels and as numerous as rabbits", they took an embarrassing interest in human affairs, and "eye-witness" accounts of their ongoings have been worth preserving if only for an evocation of daily life under elfin pressure.

"Fairies are terrible troublesome," said an old man in Fife; "they gang dancing round folk's lums, and rin through houses and play odd tricks, and lift new-born babes from their mothers. . . ." The Hawick Archaeological Society records them "riding on broomsticks round Tam Kidie's cornstack"—no doubt to his considerable discomfiture; and when observed by the coachman's wife at Yair they "nickered and leugh and danced". All highly disconcerting to douce human beings.

The fairies of the Lowland Popular Tales were so varied as to defy neat classification. Some of them, most familiar in the ballads, were human in height and appearance but hailed from a remote country known as Elphane, or Faerie,[1] from which they visited earth on hunting expeditions, sometimes carrying off such prizes as Thomas of Ercildoune or the young Tamlane. It may have been these who beat their drums before Prince Charlie's army as it marched through Jedburgh.

The "little people" were about the size of human children. They inhabited fairy hills, cheek by jowl with the villages, and were extremely familiar to their human neighbours who seem to have accepted them as part of ordinary life.

There is no doubt at all about the tenacity of the fairy belief in Scotland. James Hogg equated its strength among the peasantry with that of belief in the gospels and in fact the first printed reference to fairies "in a believing temper" occurs in John Major's *Commentary on the Gospel of St. Matthew*. Nor was credulity confined to the uneducated. Sir David Lyndsay of the Mount, Lyon King of Arms to King James V, took the matter seriously enough to state in his work on heraldry the armorial bearings appropriate to those of mixed mortal and fairy parentage —"borne of Faarie in adultré", as Michael Scot was said to have been.[2]

The post-Reformation Kirk itself was caught up in the fairy belief. The kirk session of Borgue was disturbed by their infiltration; a minister of Bedrule, the Reverend Mr. Bourland, was famed for his dealings with changelings, whom he banished with a brew of witches' thimbles picked on Ruberslaw; and the chief authority on fairy lore to this day is the Reverend Robert Kirk, son of the manse (and a seventh son, be it noted), minister of Aberfoyle in the late seventeenth century, and a graduate of both Edinburgh and Aberdeen.

Kirk was responsible for a Gaelic translation of the Psalms and an equally serious study of fairyland. His *Secret Commonwealth of Elves, Fauns and Fairies* is a thoroughly objective and careful examination of the laws and habits of a community whose existence he accepts as proven fact. He writes with scientific detachment and exactness—even on his tombstone he is described as "accurate"—but he has also a most engaging gift of description. Fairy children are "lyke enchanted puppets"; a mortal abducted to the fairy hill is replaced by a "lingering voracious image", and the embroidery work of fairy women is compared to "curious cobwebs . . . impalpable rainbows". He says, with authority, that some of the elves have "light changeable bodies (lyke those called Astral) somewhat of the nature of a cloud" and that such eat only the essence of human food which they extract, and convey to their houses by secret paths, leaving only an unsatisfying husk. Others, endowed with a more earthly nature, can be heard baking bread, striking hammers and generally behaving as mortals do.

Further south the fairies were more palpable. We have it from Allan Cunningham,[3] who carried out his researches among the old folk of Nithsdale in the early nineteenth century, that their bread tasted of honey and wine, but they also enjoyed silverweed and the tops of young heather shoots. He learned from those who claimed to have seen them that the fairies were a fair-haired race, small but well-proportioned, dressed in green mantles inlaid with wild flowers, and equipped with bog-reed arrows carried in quivers of adder skin and tipped with poison.

These were the trooping fairies, distinct from the domestic groups.

The high occasions of their year came with the Fairy Rade or Flitting. In Aberfoyle this took place on the last night of every quarter and was only visible to those with second sight. In Nithsdale the event was expected at Roodmas and warily observed by the village folk from houses protected by rowan branches. A vivid account by one who forgot to be wary is worth quoting for its language alone. Allan Cunningham got it from an old woman of Nithsdale, born about 1720:

> I' the nicht afore Roodsmass I had trysted wi' a neeber lass to talk anent buying braws i' the Fair. We had nae sutten lang aneath the hawbuss till we heard the laugh o' fowk riding, wi' the jingle o' bridles and the clank o' hoofs. We kent nae but it was fowk riding to the Fair i' the fore-nicht, but we glowered roon' an' saw it was the Fairy Fowk's Rade. We cowered doon to watch. A leam o' licht was dancing ower them mair bonny than moonshine: they were a' wee, wee fowk, wi' green scarves, but ane that rade foremaist. That ane was langer than the lave, wi' bonny lang hair bun' aboot wi' a strap whilk glented like stars. They rade on braw wee white naigs wi' unco lang swoopin' tails and manes hung wi' whustles that the wun' played on. They rade ower a high hedge o' haw-trees into a field o' corn an' gallop't into a green knowe beyont it. We gaed in the morning to look at the tredded corn, but the fient a hoof mark was there nor a blade broken.

These trooping fairies were at their most dangerous during their Rades, sometimes carrying off cattle, goods or human beings. The good neighbours, on the other hand, had hourly opportunities for tampering with village life in general, which they were not slow to use. A rashly spoken wish for help from a hard-pressed housewife could bring a fairy woman on the instant, her approach unheard—they were sometimes called "the silent ones" and were given to gliding rather than walking. Once across the threshold it took all the skill of the local wise-woman to get the too-willing helper out.

Domestic fairies lived in small family groups and were different in habits and in dress from their trooping brethren. One is described as "a little, cleanly-arrayed woman".[4] They were much given to borrowing from human neighbours—"when we have plenty they have scarcity at their house". But loans were usually repaid in good measure. A Lochmaben woman who filled a fairy's basin with meal not only got her loan back but the basin along with it,[5] and the assurance that "it would never be toom". This seems to have been quite a common experience: "The Gowan Dell" shows how profitable it could be to "obleege the fairies". For all that, however, sensible folk had no wish for "either their company or their favour".

All this coming and going must have been provoking, but the changeling business was serious. Its purpose varied. Women were

B

usually carried off as midwives or to care for children, though occasionally a fairy child might be brought to its human nurse. Abducted men were nearly always pipers or minstrels. But anyone rash enough to fall asleep on a fairy hill was asking for trouble.

A grown-up person thus snatched away had a fair chance of getting home at the end of the seven-year period when the devil's "kain" was due[6] but not surprisingly they seldom settled back into the mortal way of living. The motive for carrying off children, especially boys, was the hope that a champion of mortal birth and fairy indoctrination might one day emerge to lead the hosts of Elfland against the human kind.[7]

The ancient and infirm appearance of the elfin substitute could reasonably be put down to the reluctance of fairy mothers to part with their cherished infants, but this feature of changeling tales may have an extremely remote origin, linking the fairy belief with that of reincarnation. If, as many scholars think, the original fairies were the spirits of the dead lingering near their former homes ("what the Highlanders say of the fairies the Zulus say of the Ancestors") the wizened elf in the cradle might represent the ancestral spirit seeking re-entry into the community.

The link between the fairies and the dead is persistent and curious. It crops up in "The Miller's Tale", where the fairies' corn has to be ground on the one night of the year when the kirkyards are empty. It also accounts for the persistent tradition that fairyland is underground, and here we rouse deep echoes:

> She led him in at Eildon hill
> Underneath a dern lee,
> Where it was dark as mid-night mirk . . .[8]

The situation of fairyland, just below the earth's surface but not beyond human reach, seems to have a connection with the fairy nature, held to be lower than that of christened men but not so low as demons. According to Thomas Wilkie,[9] the fairies have always "taken notice of" a middle region and claimed that their "subterraneous abodes . . . kept them an equal distance from christened men and the devil". "Middle erd" was one of the ancient names for Elfland, and in the ballads it was the bonny road between the paths to heaven and hell— the middle way—which led to that remote and perilous country where the rain never falls.[10]

NOTES

1. "Faerie" can mean either a collective name or a state of enchantment. The early writers often used "the Fary" or "Faary" for fairyland.

2. *Armorial* 1542. The appropriate animal was a leopard. Lyndsay was appointed Lyon King of Arms in 1529.

3 See p. 141. "Some Collectors of the Tales."

4. Scott adds that they might be seen on the moors in garments dyed with lichen, which would account for the "elfin grey" of certain tales. The Hawick Archaeological Society records a glimpse of them at Ashestiel, with "black faces and wee green coaties". Sometimes they wore the local clothes: Thome Reid, a fairy man, was dressed like a Lowland small farmer. Hugh Miller's fairies appeared in tartan jerkins, long grey cloaks and red caps. (See *The Old Red Sandstone*.)

5. The basin was "of fine antique workmanship".

6. "Kain" or "cain", derived from the Gaelic cáin, meaning rent in kind, or a tax. It was a regular legal term, and there are records showing certain provisions for the levying of cain or royal tribute made in the *curia regis* at Lanark in the twelfth century. Kain cheese or fowls were paid by tenant to landlord.

This seven-yearly tribute to the devil is important in fairy-lore:

> "And never would I tire, Janet,
>   In fairy-land to dwell;
> But aye, at every seven years
>   They pay the teind to hell." . . .
>
> *Tamlane*

7. In *Folklore of Glencoe and North Lorne* Miss Barbara Fairweather writes of a girl's dress presented to the local Folk Museum, which had been worn by the donor's grandfather as a small boy by way of disguise against fairy kidnapping.

8. W. E. Aytoun, *Ballads of Scotland*. Lochs near the tops of the higher Border hills were said to be entrances to fairyland. Benighted travellers might be entangled in fairy circles and drawn down by invisible powers. (Leyden, *Scenes of Infancy*.)

9. Wilkie MS. See p. 142. "Some Collectors of the Tales."

10. A hint of this belief lingers in the Earlston tradition that True Thomas, aware that he must ultimately return to elfland, refused burial with his fathers in Earlston kirkyard "because the rain would fall upon his grave". It would be interesting to know the origin of this idea.

The Miller's Tale

Place: Galloway.
Source: *Gallovidian Annual*, No. xiv, 1933.
Narrator: The tenant of Kirkcormack Mill in 1788.
Collectors: Mr. Johnston of Kirkcudbright and Joseph Train.
  The narrator declared that he, his grandfather and his great-grandfather had all actually experienced occasions when the dead and the fairies combined to use the mill at Hallowe'en.

Ae nicht ma grandfeyther woke up wi' the sound o' the mill wheel, and being a wise-like man was for biding in his bed, but my granny, whae was an auld randy wife, gied him a clout wi' her loof and, says she, "Get up, ye donnert loon, the ghaisties and ferlies are oot."

My grandfeyther e'en did what he was telt, and cryin' on his collie he went ower to the mill to see what was up. My, but he got an unco fleg, for whit did he see but a wheen corp-claes on the grund, and around the wheel footsteps gaed back and forrit, but nae man did he see. He gaed intil the mill and the wee folk were thrang, grunin' the corn. They brocht a pickle meal and garred him taste it and they set some down to the dog, but he wadna tak' it. My grandfeyther gaed awa', no carin' to hinner the good folk, and nae sooner had he gaen through the door than it cam' to wi' a bang and smashed the puir collie's heid.

Time gaed by, an' my grandfeyther won awa', an' my granny forbye, an' my feyther was the miller o' Kirkcormack. He took nae heed o' the auld tales o' ghaists and ferlies but ae Hallowe'en[1] after he was bedded he heard the soon' o' the water and the clack o' the wheel.[2] He gaed doon in his breeks and sark for to turn it aff, but before he could dae aucht, his shouders were gruppit by someone ahint him, an' sharp pains ran through his body in stounds, as though a hunner preens was jaggin' him. He was pushed back hame wi' the grup aye on his shouders an' the cauld sweat hailed ow'er him, for weel he kenned the hands that haud him were no' the hands o' a leevin' man. An' mind ye, frae that nicht till his last hoor my feyther's shouders were aye cauld; a cauld, cauld grue was on them whilk neither fire nor lamb's wool could warm.

I was but twenty year auld when I becam' the miller mysel', an' I thocht the days o' ghaisties were bye lang syne, until there cam' a back-en' when a'thing gaed wrang about the fairm toon. The hinds kept threepin' on me to let on the mill water the hale o' yin nicht; they said that, the hairst being ower airly, the wee folk couldna wait to Hallowe'en for to get grunin' the corn, an' that they could hear them ilka nicht skreighin' an' whushin' roun' the mill dam in a wey that was awsome to harken on. Then the thorns by the dam dwyned awa' an' the fowk aboot the fairm telt me that was because the ferlies whae leeved in ablow the roots had tried to let on the water an' de'ed o't, an' the thorns they had leeved in bude to dee alang wi' them. Ae man had his leg broke in a fa' frae the laft; anither was laid by wi' the rhumatics and anither was near blin' wi' the lime frae the kiln fleein' intil his een for a' there was nae win' blawin'; an' a' the auld fowk said we bude tae gie the ferlies what they were wantin' or nae guid wad follow. But I was aye yin to gang my ain gait, an', for a' the hinnerin' o' the day's darg, I let on nae water by nicht.

At last it cam' Hallowe'en. That nicht I cried on my collie and gaed oot to the fauld nearest the kirk-yard to tak' a keek at ony ghaisties that micht be aboot. Juist on the back o' midnicht I lookit at the mill window and saw the maist oorie licht glintin' oot that e'er mortal man put e'en on.

I could feel the hair raisin' the bonnet frae my heid, but afore I could tak' a pech there cam' oot o' the door a fair-farrand looking man wi' claes on him that I had nae seen the likes o'. He loupit the kirk-yard dyke an' vanished intil the mools afore ma verra e'en. I gaed ower the dyke after him and sure as daith, juist whaur I had lost him there was an auld heid-stane pitten up tae a miller whae had dee'd in the year fifteen an seeventy-aicht. The collie had seen the ghaistie the same as mysel', an' he had got sic a gliff he rin ower the fauld, intil the hoose through a windy, an' grat like a wean in ablow the mistress's bed. An', I'm tellin' ye sooth, frae that day forrit nae mair gaed wrang aboot the fairm toon.[3]

NOTES

1. It was a firm belief in Galloway that fairy power was at its height at Hallowe'en. Lintels were hung with rowan branches and doorsteps ornamented with knots, whorls and crosses, drawn with a white "stookie" to bewilder a spirit trying to enter. But the embargo which prevented them crossing running water forced the fairies to enlist the help of the dead in grinding their corn.

2. Stone whorls, called fairy whorls, were kept in some mills and fixed at night on the spindle to keep the fairies from setting the mill going.

3. Regarding the narrator, Mr. Johnston said: "He was a most worthy pious man, and no doubt every word he uttered he believed from his very soul, for so far as we can judge human nature, the man was above deceit." Kirkcormack Mill stood on the old Kirkcudbright road about half-way between Rhonehouse and Tongland, close to Kirkcormack Kirkyard, overlooking the river Dee.

Two Changeling Tales

TIBBIE'S BAIRN

Place: Dumfriesshire.
Source: Robert Chambers, *Popular Rhymes of Scotland*.
Narrator: Charles Kirkpatrick Sharpe in the exact words of Nurse Jenny as she told the tale repeatedly during his childhood at Hoddam Castle, near Dumfries, in the seventeen-eighties.

A'body kens there's fairies, but they're no sae common now as they were langsyne. I never saw ane mysel' but my mother saw them twice—ance they had nearly drooned her when she fell asleep by the water-side: she wakened wi' them ruggin' at her hair and saw something howd doon the water like a green bunch o' potato shaws.

My mother kent a wife that lived near Dunse—they ca'ed her Tibbie Dickson. Her goodman was a gentleman's gairdner and muckle frae hame. Weel, Tibbie had a bairn, a lad bairn, just like ither bairns. Noo, Tibbie gaes ae day to the well to fetch water, and leaves the bairn in the hoose by itsel': she couldna be lang awa' for she had but to gae by the midden, and the peat-stack, and through the kail-yaird, and there stood the well.[1]

Aweel, as Tibbie was coming back wi' her water, she hears a

skirl in her hoose like the stickin' o' a gryse or the singin' o' a soo: fast she rins and flies to the cradle and there, I wat, she saw a sicht that made her heart scunner. In place o' her ain bonny bairn she fand a withered wolron, naething but skin and bane, wi' haunds like a moudiewart and a face like a paddock, a mouth frae lug to lug and twa great glowerin' een.[2]

When Tibbie saw sic a daft-like bairn she scarce kent what to do or whether it was her ain or no. Whiles she thocht it was a fairy, whiles that some ill een had sp'ilt her wean when she was at the well. It wad never sook, but suppit mair parritch in ae day than twa herd callants could do in a week. It was aye yammerin' and greetin' but never minded to speak a word; and when ither bairns could rin it couldna stand. Sae Tibbie was sair fashed aboot it, as it lay in its cradle at the fireside like a half-deid hurcheon.

Tibbie had span some yarn to make a wab and the wabster lived at Dunse, so she maun gae there; but there was naebody to look after the bairn. Weel, her neist neighbour was a tylor; they ca'ed him Wullie Grieve: he had a humpit back but he was a tap tylor for a' that—he cloutit a pair o' breeks for my faither when he was a boy. So Tibbie goes to the tylor and says: "Wullie, I maun awa' to Dunse aboot ma wab and I dinna ken what to do wi' the bairn till I come back; ye ken it's but a whingin', screech-in', skirlin' wallidreg—but we maun bear wi' dispensations. I wad wuss ye," quo' she, "to tak' tent till't till I come hame. Ye sall hae a roosin' ingle and a blast o' the goodman's tobacco-pipe forbye."

Wullie was naething laith, and back they gaed thegither.

Wullie sits doon at the fire and awa' wi' her yarn gaes the wife; but scarce had she steekit the door and wan hauf-way doon the close when the bairn cocks up on its doup in the cradle and rounds in Wullie's lug: "Wullie Tylor, an ye winna tell my mither when she comes back, I'se play ye a bonny spring on the bag-pipes."

I wat Wullie's heart was like to loup the hool—for tylors, ye ken, are aye timorsome; but he thinks to himsel': "Fair fashions are still best"; an' "It's better to fleetch fules than to flyte wi' them"; sae he rounds again in the bairn's lug: "Play up, my doo, an' I'se tell naebody."

Wi' that the fairy ripes amang the cradle strae and pu's oot a pair o' pipes, sic as tylor Wullie ne'er had seen in a' his days—

muntit wi' ivory and gold and siller and dymonts, and what not. I dinna ken what spring the fairy played but this I ken weel, that Wullie had nae great good o' his performance; so he sits thinkin' to himsel': "This maun be a deil's get;[3] and I ken weel hoo to treat them; and gin I while the time awa' Auld Waughorn himsel' may come to rock his ain's cradle and play me some foul prank"; sae he catches the bairn by the cuff o' the neck and whups him into the fire, bagpipes and a'.

"*Fuff*"—

Awa' flees the fairy skirlin', "Deil stick the lousy tylor!" a' the way up the lum.[4]

RIDDLING IN THE REEK

Place: Galloway.
Source: *Gallovidian Annual*, No. xi, 1909.
  "Superstitious Record in the South-West of Scotland", J. Maxwell Wood.
  "A realistic account" preserved in Wigtownshire.

A child whose parents lived in Sorbie village behaved in such a fretful, passionate, and vixenish way that the parents were at last forced to the unwelcome conclusion that it was not their child at all, but a changeling. Much distressed, they sought the advice of a wise woman living at Kirkinner who promised to make an attempt to restore the child on the following Aul' Hallowe'en Nicht.

When Aul' Hallowe'en cam' everything was ready and set in order, and just a few minutes before nine, in came Lucky McRobert and, without saying a word, steekit the door ahint her.

She set two stools beside the fire, which was made on a slightly raised place in the middle of the floor, paved with water stones. Beckoning to the parents to sit on these, she lit the candle with the ether-stane, put it on the kerl, or long candlestick, and set it between them. Then she took rowan wood and biggit it on the fire.

The wean looked terrified and ran under the bed, but she pulled him oot, tied his legs and arms together wi' red clouts she had in her pooch, threw him into the riddle and carried it towards the fire, the wean twining and kicking and swearing most viciously.

Lucky had breeked her petticoats, and as soon as a thick reek rose from the burning rowan-tree, she held the wean amang the thickest o't and riddled it in the riddle till ye wud hae thocht it wud hae been chokit.

The wean cursed and yelled and spat at her a' that was bad, but she took nae notice; then it begged and fleech't with the faither and mother to save't, for it was chokin' and went on pitifu'; and then it begood and cursed them and abused them terribly.

Then there came knockings to the door, and cries and noisings all over the house; but she aye riddled away and naebody heeded, till at last the wean gave a great scraich and rase oot o' the riddle and gaed whirling up amang the reek like a corkscrew, and oot at the lumhead, oot o' sicht.

Everything was quiet then for a minute or two, till at last a gentle knocking came to the door and Lucky asked who was there. A voice cried, "Let me in, I'm wee Tammie."

NOTES

1. The lay-out of a Lowland farm-toun before the agrarian revolution is interesting.

2. According to Lewis Spence, the marks of a changeling were "its wan and wrinkled appearance, its long fingers and slightly bony development . . . its fractious behaviour and voracious appetite. In Scotland its large teeth and fondness for music and dancing usually betrayed it." In doubtful cases it sometimes fell to the minister to make the final judgement.

3. . . .—in other words, the devil's kain (see note 6, p. 5). They were sometimes called kain bairns.

4. The last resort was to threaten burning. The chances were that a changeling thrown into the fire would vanish up the chimney and the genuine child would reappear (as in "Riddling the Reek"). The days before baptism were the danger time and the commonest safeguards were fire and cold iron. As late as the sixteenth century some midwives still carried fire in a circle round mother and baby, night and morning. Sometimes a smoothing iron was kept in the bed. Edward Clodd suggests that iron would be an unknown and therefore dangerous substance to witches and fairies, who belonged to the Stone Age. In Fife a pair of men's breeches were often folded and laid under the mother's head for the first three nights after the birth. After the baby's first sneeze the danger of fairy interference was less.

The Fairies in Need

"NURSE KIND AND NE'ER WANT"

Place: Nithsdale.
Source: R. H. Cromek, *Remains of Galloway and Nithsdale Song.*
Collector: Alan Cunningham.

A young woman of Nithsdale was singing and rocking her child when a lady came into the cottage wearing a fairy mantle. She carried a beautiful child swaddled in green silk.

"Gie my bonnie thing a sook," says the Fairy.

The young woman took the child kindly and the Fairy instantly disappeared, saying "Nurse kind and ne'er want."

The young mother cared for the two children. When she awoke in the morning she would often find rich clothing for them both and delicious food, which tasted like loaf mixed with wine and honey and kept fresh for seven days.

On the approach of summer the Fairy came again and the child bounded with joy at the sight of her. Delighted with its vigour, she took it in her arms and, bidding the nurse follow, led the way through some scroggy woods and half way up the sunward slope of a green hill, where a door opened. They entered a porch and the door closed behind them.

The Fairy dropped three drops of dew on the nurse's left eyelid and they entered a land watered with looping rivers and yellow with corn. The nurse was given webs of fine cloth, salves for restoring mortal health and the promise of never needing. When the Fairy dropped a green dew in her right eye she was able to see many of her lost friends reaping the corn and gathering fruit— the punishment of their evil deeds. Then the Fairy passed a hand over her eye, restoring its ordinary sight, and led her back to the porch; but not before she had secured a box of the green dew.

For many years the woman had the gift of seeing earth-visiting spirits; but one day she met the Fairy from whom she had stolen the green dew, and greeted her.

"What e'e d'ye see me wi'?" whispered the Fairy.

"Wi' them baith."

The Fairy breathed on her eyes, whereupon the power of the green dew failed, and was never restored.

A BACK-GAEN WEAN

Place: Galloway.
Source: *Dumfries and Galloway Naturalist and Antiquarian Society*, Transactions, 1912-13.
Narrator: "A Whithorn woman of great age, still a believer in fairies."

Ae morning a wee body cam' tae the door and asked me if I could gie her a wee drap o' milk for a back-gaen[1] wean. I said I wad look and see if I had ony, if she wad just haud ma wean a meenit.

"Na, na," quo' she; "I'll no haud yer wean, but if ye pit her in the cradle I'll look after her till ye come back." Sae I gaed for the milk.

She thankit me a lot, and then said: "Ye're a nice sonsy body, an' as lang as ye leeve ye'll ne'er ken want."

NOTE

1. Back-gaen usually means that the sufferer has had "a waff o' the evil eye" —but surely not in the case of a fairy's child!

NAE SARK FOR THE BAIRN

Place: Roxburghshire.
Source: *Transactions of the Hawick Archeological Society.*

The fairies around Ruberslaw had a high character for gratitude.

A poor man from Jedburgh, on his way to Hawick sheep market, heard women's voices wailing and howling but no-one was visible and all the words he could gather were, "O there's a bairn born but there's nae sark to put on't."

He stripped off his shirt and threw it on the ground. An invisible hand snatched it up, the wailing stopped and there was laughter.

The man buttoned up his coat, marched to Hawick, bought his mert and went home. From that day all he did prospered.

A Wyf to Sandy Harg

Place: Nithsdale.
Source: R. H. Cromek, *Remains of Galloway and Nithsdale Song.*
Collector: Allan Cunningham.

Alexander Harg, a cottar in the parish of New Abbey, had courted and married a pretty girl whom the Fairies had long attempted to seduce from this world. A few nights after his marriage he was standing with a halve-net awaiting the approach of the tide. Two old vessels stranded on the rocks were visible at mid-water mark and were believed to be haunts of the Fairies when crossing the mouth of the Nith. In one of these wrecks a loud noise was heard, as of carpenters at work; a hollow voice cried from the other:

"Ho, what're ye doing?"

"I'm making a wyf to Sandy Harg."

The husband, astonished and terrified, threw down his net, hastened home, closed every door and window and seized his wife in his arms.

At midnight a gentle rap came to the door, with a most courteous three times touch. The girl started to get up, but Sandy held her.

A footstep was heard departing and instantly the cattle lowed and bellowed, ramping as if pulling up their stakes. The horses pranced, neighed and snorted. She cried, struggled and entreated, but he would not move. The noise and tumult increased, but died away with the dawn.

In the morning Sandy Harg found a piece of moss oak fashioned to the shape and size of his wife propped against the garden dyke.

Gilpin Horner

Place: Borders.
Source: Sir Walter Scott, *The Lay of the Last Minstrel* (Notes).
Narrator: "A man called Anderson" born and bred at Todshaw-
hill in Eskdalemuir. He told the story to a friend of Scott, saying
that he had often heard his father speak of the incident with complete belief.

Late one evening, when it was growing dark, two men were
fastening their horses[1] upon the uttermost part of their ground,
when they heard a voice crying, "Tint! Tint! Tint!"

One of the men, Moffat by name, called out, "What deil has
tint ye? Come here!" Immediately a creature of something like
human form appeared. It was surprisingly little, distorted in
features and mis-shapen in limbs.

As soon as the two men had seen it they ran home in a great
fright, imagining they had met with some goblin. By the way
Moffat fell and it ran over him and was home at the house as soon
as either of them. It stayed there a long time, but I cannot say
how long. It was real flesh and blood and ate and drank, was fond
of cream and—when it could get at it—would destroy a great deal.

It seemed a mischievous creature; and any of the children it
could master it would beat and scratch without mercy. It was
once abusing a child belonging to the same Moffat who had been
so frightened by its first appearances and he, in a passion, struck
it so violent a blow on the side of the head that it tumbled on the
ground, but it was not stunned, for it set up its head directly and
exclaimed, "Ah-hah, Will o' Moffat, you strike sair!"

After it had stayed there long, one evening when the women
were milking the cows in the loan it was playing among the
children near by them, when suddenly they heard a loud shrill
voice near by cry three times, "Gilpin Horner!"

It started and said, "That is me, I must away," and instantly
disappeared.

Besides constantly repeating the word "tint", Gilpin Horner
was often heard to call upon Peter Be-te-ram. When the shrill
voice called it was the summons of Peter Bertram, who seems to
have been the devil who had lost the little imp.

[The narrator adds, "I can only say that no legend I have ever heard seemed to be more universally credited."]

NOTE

1. The custom was to tie the horse's forefeet together to keep it from straying in the night. This was also a means of tethering cattle, as in "A Wyf to Sandy Harg".

A Fairy Joke

Place: Galloway.
Source: *The Castle Douglas Miscellany*, vol. 2.

Draw thy stool nearer and I'll tell ye a true tale that happened when I was a bit gilpin o' a lassie at Lochinwhirn.

My cousin Maggie Fairgray was as sonsie a weel-faured lass as ever graced the Ha' o' ony farmer atween Gargen Brig and the Corse o' Slakes. She wasna brought up like the guid-for-naething hizzies nowadays. A' the time Maggie could be spared frae the hay or the peat moss she gave to tentin' her daddie's sheep.

Well, it happened on a fine afternoon about auld Lammas as Maggie sat spinning on her rock[1] on a mickle grey stane near the brow o' the well that bears her name to this day, she happened to look towards the well and frae a stump o' moss oak about a foot ablow the water she saw gold chains supporting a kettle as large as ever swung in Lizzie Lowne's lodging house.

Awa' she hied wi' a' speed for her faither and brithers, but first she stuck up her rock—spindle and tow—to mark the place. I mind weel to see her coming a' forfochten up the close, crying, "Faither, Jamie, Will, every ane o' ye, come awa' to the well at the back o' Bodsknowe and help me out wi' a pot o' gowd I saw in't."

"Hout, daft lassie," quo' her faither, "ye hae either been dreamin' or some Elfe has casten its glamour o'er ye to gar ye droon yersel' in that unsonsie well, but howsomever I'm thankfu' ye hae escaped sae weel; and noo we'll gang and see this wonderfu' sight o' yours, though troath I doubt nane o' us will be muckle the richer o't."

When they reached the tap o' the hill and Maggie cast her

e'en towards Bodsknowe to look for her rock and spindle, the whole mosses and moors as far as they could see was a forest of rocks and spindles.

"Did I no tell ye," quo' her faither, "that it was a fairy concern a'thegether? And look yonders, the verra fowk themsel's!"

Wi' that a dozen wee fowk clad in green, as wi' ae voice, started the auld sang, "Tea and Brandy," then cried, "Maggie, Maggie, look aboot! Look aboot!"

Maggie and her friends did sae, and when they turned round again the elfin singers had set up a loud laugh and vanished. Maggie's rock was lying at her feet, the whole valley had its usual appearance, but her hale stock o' tow was spun up.

And that's nae carried clash, for it happened amang my ain honest fowks that wadna lie for naebody.

NOTE

1. Rock is a distaff—a cleft staff about three feet long. The single word can be used, as here, to include the quantity of wool or flax wound round it, ready for spinning.

A Fairy Invitation

Place: Galloway.
Source: Letter to Joseph Train from Robert Malcolmson of Kirkcudbright, July 1820. Unpublished MS. National Library of Scotland.
    "This story was told by the man's wife to one of her friends whose grandson related it to me."

There lived, upwards of a century ago at the Woolcoats, a wild and lonely place in Annandale, a family between whom and the fairies the most friendly intercourse subsisted. One time, the fairies invited the goodman of the house to a wedding.

They conveyed him to the place, which appeared to be a large and elegant hall where there were feasting and music and dancing. They were all dressed in green and had small caps on their heads, and they presented their guest with a cap exactly like their own, telling him not to take it off his head on any account whatsoever.

In the course of the evening, in compliance with one of their

C

own established customs, all the fairies took off their caps. Forgetting his instructions, the stranger removed his and immediately fell to the ground. On rising up, to his astonishment, he found himself in his own barn.

Sir Godfrey McCulloch

Place: Galloway.
Source: Sir Walter Scott, *Minstrelsy of the Scottish Border*.

As Sir Godfrey McCulloch was taking the air on horseback near his own house, he was suddenly accosted by a little old man arrayed in green and mounted upon a white palfrey. After mutual salutation, the old man gave Sir Godfrey to understand that he resided under his house and that he had great reason to complain of a drain or common sewer which emptied itself directly on to his chamber of dais.[1]

Sir Godfrey was a good deal startled at this extraordinary complaint; but guessing the nature of the being he had to deal with, he assured the old man with great courtesy that the direction of the drain would be altered, and caused this to be done.[2]

Many years afterwards, Sir Godfrey had the misfortune to kill, in a fray, a gentleman of the neighbourhood.[3] He was apprehended, tried and condemned. The scaffold on which his head was to be struck off was erected on the Castle-hill of Edinburgh, but hardly had he reached the fatal spot when the old man on his white palfrey pressed through the throng with the rapidity of lightning. At his command Sir Godfrey sprang on behind him; the "good neighbour" spurred his horse down the steep bank, and neither he nor Sir Godfrey was ever seen again.

NOTES

1. In the fifteenth and sixteenth centuries a long table was usually set across one end of the hall of a Scottish castle. "This table is known as the 'hie burd', and it stands on a dais some inches higher than the rest of the floor, being reserved for the use of the more important guests . . . the lord of the castle sits in a high-backed chair in the middle, and if he observes great state, there may be a canopy suspended from the ceiling above his seat. On his right and left are the guests. . . ." See John Warrack, *Domestic Life in Scotland, 1488-1688*.

2. A shepherd's wife in a lonely onstead in the Galloway hills often found a "wee body" on her doorstep borrowing odds and ends and disappearing with suspicious speed. One day when the goodwife was at the door emptying dirty water, the visitor approached. "Goodwife," said she, "ye're really a very obliging body. Wad ye be sae good as turn the lade o' your jaw-hole anither way, as a' your foul water rins through my door. It stands in the howe there on the aff-side o' that tree at the corner o' your house en'."

The tree, it appeared, hid the entrance to the fairy hill.

3. This at least coincides with fact. Sir Godfrey's trial took place in 1697.

Another account of Sir Godfrey's adventures is worth quoting. The extract is from a letter to Scott, dated March 1817, from Joseph Train:

"You will no doubt be already well acquainted with the story of Sir Godfrey shooting the Laird of Bushabiel before the door of the latter in a dispute about the trespass of their cattle. A red mark is pointed out on a stone to this day, as being the blood of the unfortunate laird.

"To escape the punishment incurred by such a crime Sir Godfrey fled to the Continent where he remained for many years till at last young Bushabiel, the son of the old man, assured the Knight's friends that he might return to his native country with safety as no more notice would be taken of the unhappy affray.

"Sir Godfrey had no sooner returned to Galloway than Bushabiel invited him in a most friendly manner to a feast he meant to give in honour of his return, that he might show in the most public manner how sincerely he could forgive and forget an injury.

"Sir Godfrey was prevented from accepting the invitation by a prophetic dream. It was really the intention of Bushabiel to decoy him to the place where his father had been shot, and murder him; and finding that his design had failed, he raised his followers and they surrounded the Castle of Cardoness at midnight. Rightly judging their intention, Sir Godfrey escaped by a secret passage but was closely pursued all the way to Edinburgh where he was taken into St. Giles' church during the time of Sermon, and afterwards suffered the punishment of the Law."

The Gowan Dell

Place: Clackmannan.
Source: *County Folklore* (Clackmannan) 1914.
Narrator: "An old woman who lived in the Dell."
Collector: J. B. Simkins.

It's mony years since the awfu' drooth happened to this kintra which turned a' oor bonnie green hills and fields as broon as a docken and as dry as poother. Everything was quite withered and the thing appeared sae judgement-like that some fasted or prayed and ithers were thrown into a state bordering on despair. The verra burns and wells were nearly a' dried up.

This drooth continued for twa months, in which time a great mony fine kye died, and likewise sheep; and sma' farmers were reduced to a state o' perfect poverty.

The fairies, puir bodies, did a' in their po'er to assist the distressed, and it was strange that their rings and hillocks never suffered in the least frae the heat but remained fresh and green.

In this sad time there was a man o' the name o' Sandy Crawford, wha had obleeged the fairies on several occasions; and weel can thae folk repay a benefit, and weel can they avenge an injury. He was a good man, for he could never bear to see his fellow creatures want, and as lang as he had a bawbee to spare he never held his hand. His three kye had perished, and they being his means o' supporting his wife and family, it was nae wonder he became sae dooncast.

As he was sitting ae nicht by the side o' the fire efter a' the family had been bedded, a hugger[1] cam' doon the lum and fell at his feet. He opened it, and his astonishment was great when he found it fu' o' gowd pieces. At the foot was a sma' piece o' paper wi' this inscription:

> Tak' the gowd and buy a coo—
> You minded us, we've minded you.

Next morning Sandy trudged awa', without telling his wife onything aboot it, to a rich farmer aboot Kinross whaur he laid out part o' his siller in buying twa fine kye, which he brocht hame. But he hadna considered hoo they were to be kept.

But the fairies soon settled the matter, for they tell't him to drive them to the Dell, which at that time was a' covered wi' rashes, whins and briars. Sandy kent the place fu' weel, and was gaun to laugh at the proposal, but hafflins afraid lest he should offend those wha had been sae guid to him, he drave his twa kye awa' to the Dell.

If he was surprised at the gowd, he was quite dumfoondered at the changed look o' the place. Every bush and weed had disappeared and in their stead had sprung up a beautiful crop o' the richest and finest grass.

The twa kye gaed here week after week and still there was no sign o' the grass withering or growing bare. Each o' the kye yielded atween saxteen and auchteen pints o' milk a day,[2] and the butter frae it surpassed onything o' its kind. The fame o't spread far and wide and folk cam' frae a' the airts to get it.

The neighbours began to grow jealous and soon Sandy had mony enemies wha, thinkin' they wad get on as weel as him, turned their kye into the Dell. But what did it matter? Not a single coo but Sandy Crawford's ga'e a drap o' milk!

The drooth ended and showers fell again, sae that the kintra began to recover. Sandy Crawford gaed on prosperously in the warld, never fa'in' back a day. As for the Gowan Dell, it has just the self and same appearance enoo as it had that morning when the twa kye o' Sandy's first set fit within it.

NOTES

1. A hugger was an old stocking leg used as a pouch for money, usually hoarded savings. There is an overtone of secrecy—in Galloway "hugger muggering" meant doing business not openly. A form of proposing marriage might be: "Your hugger and my hugger coupit intil ane, wad be sure to keep us confartable as lang's we leeve."

2. By way of comparison, Carlyle declares that at Craigenputtock their own cow gave 27 quarts of milk daily in the two or three best months of the summer. (*Reminiscences: Essay on Jane Welsh Carlyle.*)

The Goodwife of Wastness

Place: Orkney.
Source: *County Folklore* (Orkney and Shetland) 1903.
Narrator: A native of North Ronaldsay.
Collector: G. F. Black.

The goodman of Wastness was well-to-do, a good-looking well-favoured man with a well-stocked farm, and though many braw lasses in the island had set their caps at him, he was not to be caught. When urged by his friends to take a wife, he would say, "If that ould fool Adam had not been bewitched by his wife, he might have been a happy man in the yard of Edin till this day." The old wife of Longer, who heard him, said, "Take doo heed de sell, doo'll may be de sell bewitched some day." "Aye," quoth he, "that will be when doo walks dry shod frae the Alters o' Seenie to dae Boar of Papa."

Well, it happened one day that the good-man of Wastness was down on the ebb when he saw, at a little distance, a number of selkie folk on a flat rock. Some were lying sunning themselves, while others jumped and played about in great glee. They were all naked and had skins as white as his own. The rock on which they sported had deep water on its seaward side, and on its shore side a shallow pool.

The goodman of Wastness crept unseen till he got to the edge of the shallow pool; he then rose and dashed through the pool to the rock. The selkie folk seized their skins and, in mad haste, jumped into the sea. Quick as they were, the goodman was quick also, and he seized one of the skins belonging to an unfortunate girl who, in her terror, had left it as she sprang into the water.

The selkie folk swam out a little distance, then turning, set up their heads and gazed at the goodman. He noticed that one of them had not the appearance of seals like the rest, and taking the captured skin under his arm he made for home. Before he had got out of the ebb he heard the most doleful sound of lamentation behind him, and turned to see a fair woman following him. She was a pitiful sight; sobbing and holding out both hands in supplication; and ever and anon she cried out, "O bonnie man, if there's ony mercy i' thee human breast, gae back me skin! I canno', canno', canno' live i' the sea without it. I canno', canno', bide among me ain folk without me ain seal skin. O, pity a puir distressed forlorn lass, gin doo wad ever hope for mercy theesel'."

The goodman was not too soft-hearted, yet he could not help pitying her, and with pity came love. His heart that never loved woman before was conquered by the beauty of the sea-lass, and he wrung from her reluctant consent to live with him as his wife. She chose this as the least of two evils. Without the skin she could not live in the sea, and he absolutely refused to give it up.

So the sea-lass went with the goodman and stayed with him,

being a thrifty, frugal and kindly goodwife. She bore her goodman seven children, four boys and three lasses, and there were
not bonnier lasses or statelier boys in all the isle. And though the

goodwife of Wastness appeared happy, and was sometimes merry,
yet there seemed at times to be a weight on her heart, and many a
longing look did she fix on the sea. She taught her bairns many a

strange song that nobody on earth had ever heard before. Albeit she was a thing of the sea, yet the goodman led a happy life with her.

Now it chanced one day that the goodman of Wastness and his three elder sons were off in his boat to the fishing. The goodwife sent three of the other children to the ebb to gather limpets and wilks. The youngest lass had to stay at home for she had a beelan foot. The goodwife then began, under the pretence of house cleaning, a determined search for her long lost skin.

She searched up and she searched down; she searched but and she searched ben; she searched out and she searched in, but never a skin could she find, while the sun wore to the west. The youngest lass sat on a stool with her foot on a cringlo. She says to her mother, "Mam, what are doo leukan for?" "O bairn, deu no tell," said her mother, "but I'm leukan for a bonnie skin, tae mak a rivlin that wad ceur thee sare fit."

Says the lass, "May be I ken whar hid is. Ae day whin ye were a' oot, an' Ded thought I was sleepan i' the bed, he took a bonnie skin doon; he glowred at it a peerie minute, dan folded hid and led hid up under dae aisins abeun dae bed."

When her mother heard this she rushed to the place and pulled out her skin.

"Fareweel, peerie buddo!" said she to the child and ran out. She rushed to the shore, flung on her skin and plunged into the sea with a wild cry of joy. A male of the selkie folk met her with every sign of delight.

The goodman was rowing home and saw them both. His lost wife uncovered her face and cried to him: "Goodman o' Wastness, fareweel tae thee! I liked dee weel; doo war geud tae me; bit I lo'e better me man o' the sea."

And that was the last he ever saw or heard of his bonnie wife.

II

THE ROUGH FAIRIES

THIS shaggy, mis-shapen race left such an impact on rural life and were so obstinately and outlandishly individual in habit and appearance that they deserve a section to themselves.

Chief among them was the Brownie, so called for his swarthy colour but on no account to be confused with the Brown Man of the Muir, whose delight was to terrify and if possible to harm the human race. The latter takes his place with such malevolent spirits as the kelpie,[1] Shelleycoat, Redcap of the terrible laugh and the three goblins who held "hellish orgies" by night at the three thorns of Carlinwark.[2]

The Brownie was kindly disposed and capable of real devotion to the family he chose to serve. Descended from the Roman domestic gods, he has also a very respectable tradition in Christian literature, going back in Scotland to John Major's *Commentary on the Gospel of St. Matthew* ("isti fauni invocati brobne; qui non nocent . . .") and in Europe to St. Augustine's *City of God*; but Scott's description in *Redgauntlet* of Crystal Nixon might have been written of him—"thick, short, shaggy and hirsute as a lion".

Once attached to an agricultural family, the Brownie became a faithful servant in kitchen, steading and field and all for a cogful of brose and milk; though an occasional small extra was not refused— knuckled cakes made of meal warm from the mill, haurned in the embers and spread with honey.[3] "*There's* a piece would please a Brownie!" To offer him money or clothing was to give him his marching orders

> Gie Brownie coat, gie Brownie sark
> Ye's get nae mair o' Brownie's wark

but this was seldom done except in ignorance, though a certain old woman in Ettrick forest did deliberately "hire away" the local Brownie with a coin left beside his porringer. He howled his farewell throughout a whole night, but he had to go.

Working while men slept, the Brownie had the right to take his meal by the midnight hearth after the family and servants were bedded, blowing up the dying embers with the pluff[4] and stretching his weary length in their warmth. Not surprisingly, he was impatient with late bedders and might even hasten them with a rebuke: "Get ye a' gane to your beds, sirs, and dinna pit oot the wee grieshoch."

Children could safely be left in the care of this uncouth but faithful servant and according to Wilkie he was often appointed guardian of money yirded by a hunted man, an expedient which probably accounts for finds of "fairy gold" in later centuries.[5]

The Doonie, who frequented Nithsdale and the Borders, may have been a Danish version of the Brownie.[6] Certainly they were much alike in character and habits, the main difference being that while the Brownie never assumed any shape but his own, the Doonie might appear as an old man or woman, or even as a pony, in which guise he came to the rescue of one McMath, a Nithsdale herd, as he struggled through a wild December night of the eighteenth century in search of a doctor for his wife. An inferior member of the same family was the Dobie, well-meaning if stupid; but a group of highly original characters each with a distinctive name and often associated with one particular place, can be fitted into this class of fairy.

The cow-lug spirits, for instance, were to be seen on Cowlugs' E'en at Bowden and Gattonside, and nowhere else, and Bowden also supported Wag-at-the-Wa' who enlivened its kitchens by swinging on the crook after the pot was off the fire. An old woman described him to Wilkie as "a grizzlt-headed old man with yill-cap e'en, a mouth full of broken stumps, and one very long hooked front tooth, which he kept hooked to his ear". He had short crooked legs, long hairy arms and a tail by which he hung on the swee. Human company greatly pleased him and when jokes went round his laughter could be heard, but to invite him into the circle by wagging the crook was to commit the sin of "invokerie", and to this day old crooks may be found in the Borders incised with a cross, which kept him from his sport. When at home he wore a grey mantle and pirnie-cap, much blackened by smoke, but his marching dress was gay—red coat, blue breeches and stockings of good Fairnilee wool.

Kitchen-loving and—unlike the ordinary fairy—fearless of fire, Wag-at-the-Wa', despite his Fairnilee stockings, has too much in common with the Roman Lar to pass for a native Borderer. Remembering how close Bowden lies to the site of Trimontium, it is easy to picture him slipping over the shoulder of the Eildons to this snug refuge as the Legions marched away.[7]

NOTES

1. The kelpie frequented rivers and lochs and the larger burns, in the form of a cow, a horse, a youth or a girl, and always with malevolent intent,

though a Buittle woman, washing pudding skins in the burn after a pig-killing, had a pleasant encounter with one:

"What gars ye look sae dowie the day?" says the kelpie.

"Eh," says the guidwife, "I bude to flit frae my biggin' come Martinmas an' I'm gey sweir to gang."

"Hoots," says the kelpie, "dinna fash yersel' for that. Ye'll wash puddin' skins in this burn the next twenty year gin ye aye pit oot a pickle brose on Hallowe'en."

2. Letter to Sir Walter Scott from Joseph Train. See p. 139. "Some Collectors of the Tales."

3. Since the Brownie tended the bees he deserved his share of the honey, particularly in Galloway where Borgue honey was far famed. "In London", Mactaggart records with pride, "there is a sign with 'Borgue hinnie for ever', wrote on it."

4. The pluff was a hollowed-out stem of boor-tree (elder) used as bellows.

5. Dr. Robert Simpson suggests that some of the seventeenth-century Brownies may have been Covenanters on the run, sheltered through the winter by friendly farmers and showing their gratitude by working through the night. "None of the domestics to whom the secret had not been committed by the master durst approach the scene of their operations. There was an eeriness about the thing and an uncomfortable idea that the place was haunted; and this helped to keep the secret. The farmer would have been found guilty of reset had the thing been known, and punished accordingly; and that punishment was not light. . . . It happily never occurred to the persecutors to suspect that the Brownies were anything else than what popular belief had assigned them." (Robert Simpson, *The Cottars of the Glen.*)

6. See R. De B. Trotter, *"Galloway Superstitions"*.

7. Scott reminds us that Roman mythology included "a certain species of subordinate deities resembling the modern elves in their habits", and recalls how Mr. Gibb of the Advocates Library would point to the inscription "Diis campestribus" on a Roman altar found near Roxburgh Castle with the remark, "the fairies, ye ken". (*Letters on Demonology and Witchcraft.* Letter III.)

The Brownie of Blednoch

Place: Galloway.
Source: William Nicholson, *Tales in Verse and Miscellaneous Poems*.

Dr. John Brown considered this poem comparable to Tam o' Shanter in its union of the comic, the pathetic and the terrible. "Here is the indescribable, inestimable, unmistakable impress of genius."

There cam' a strange wight to our town-en',
And the fient a body did him ken;
He tirled na lang, but he glided ben
    Wi' a dreary, dreary hum.

His face did glare like the glow o' the west
When the drumlie cloud has it half o'ercast;
Or the struggling moon when she's sad distrest—
    O sirs! 'Twas Aiken-drum.

I trow the bauldest stood aback
Wi' a gape and a glower till their lugs did crack,
An' the shapeless phantom mum'ling spak',
    "Hae ye wark for Aiken-drum?"

O had ye seen the bairns' fright
As they stared at this wild and unyirthly wight
As he stauket in 'tween the dark and light
    And graned out, "Aiken-drum!"

"Sauf us!" quoth Jock, "d'ye see sic een!"
Cries Kate, "there's a hole where a nose should hae been
And the mouth's like a gash which a horn had ri'en;
    Wow! keep's frae Aiken-drum!"

The black dog growling cowered his tail,
The lassie swarfed, loot fa' the pail;
Rob's lingle brak as he men't the flail
    At the sight o' Aiken-drum.

His matted head on his breist did rest,
A lang blue beard wan'ered down like a vest;
But the glare o' his e'en nae bard hath exprest,
   Nor the skimes o' Aiken-drum.

Roun' his hairy form there was naething seen
But a philabeg o' the rashes green,[1]
And his knotted knees played aye knoit between;
   What a sight was Aiken-drum!

On his wauchie arms three claws did meet
As they trailed on the grun' by his taeless feet;
E'en the auld gudeman himsel' did sweat
   To look at Aiken-drum.

But he drew a score, himsel' did sain;
The auld wife tried, but her tongue was gane;
While the young ane closer clasped her wean
   And turned frae Aiken-drum.

But the canny auld wife cam' till her breath,
And she deemed the Bible might ward aff scaith,
Be it benshee, bogle, ghaist or wraith—[2]
   But it fear't na Aiken-drum.

"His presence protect us!" quoth the auld gudeman;
"What wad ye, where won ye—by sea or by lan'?
I conjure ye—speak—by the Beuk in my han'!"
   What a grane ga'e Aiken-drum!

"I lived in a lan' where we saw nae sky,
I dwelt in a spot where a burn rins na by;
But I'se dwall now wi' you if ye like to try—
   Ha'e ye wark for Aiken-drum?

"I'll shiel a' your sheep i' the mornin' sune,[3]
I'll berry your crap by the light o' the moon,
And baa the bairns wi' an unken'd tune
   If ye'll keep puir Aiken-drum.

"I'll loup the linn when ye canna wade,
I'll kirn the kirn, and I'll turn the bread,
And the wildest fillie that ever ran rede,
   I'se tame't," quoth Aiken-drum!

"To wear the tod frae the flock on the fell—
To gather the dew frae the heather bell—
And to look at my face in your clear crystal well
   Might gie pleasure to Aiken-drum.

"I'se seek nae guids, gear, bond nor mark;
I use nae beddin', shoon nor sark;
But a cogfu' o' brose 'tween the light and dark
   Is the wage o' Aiken-drum."

Quoth the wylie auld wife, "The thing speaks weel;
Our workers are scant—we hae routh o' meal;
Giff he'll do as he says—be he man, be he de'il,
   Wow! we'll try this Aiken-drum."

But the wenches skirled, "He's no be here!
His eldritch look gars us swarf wi' fear,
And the fient a ane will the house come near
   If they think but o' Aiken-drum.

For a foul and a stalward ghaist is he
Despair sits brooding aboon his e'e bree,
And unchancie to light o' a maiden's e'e
   Is the grim glower o' Aiken-drum."

"Puir slipmalabours! ye ha'e little wit;
Is't na hallowmas now, and the crap out yet?"
Sae she silenced them a' wi' a stamp o' her fit;
   "Sit yer wa's down, Aiken-drum."

Roun' a' that side what wark was done
By the streamer's gleam or the glance o' the moon;
A word or a wish—and the brownie cam' sune,
   Sae helpfu' was Aiken-drum.

But he slade aye awa' ere the sun was up;
He ne'er could look straught on Macmillan's cup,[4]
They watched—but nane saw him his brose ere sup,
   Nor a spune sought Aiken-drum.

On Blednoch's banks and on crystal Cree
For mony a day a toiled wight was he;
While the bairnies played harmless roun' his knee,
   Sae social was Aiken-drum.

But a new-made wife, fu' o' rippish freaks,
Fond o' a' things feat for the first five weeks,
Laid a mouldy pair o' her ain man's breeks
   By the brose o' Aiken-drum.

Let the learned decide when they convene
What spell was him and the breeks between;
For frae that day forth he was nae mair seen,
   And sair missed was Aiken-drum.

He was heard by a herd gaun by the Threive,
Crying, "Lang, lang now may I greet and grieve;
For alas! I ha'e gotten baith fee and leave,
   O luckless Aiken-drum!"

Awa! ye wrangling sceptic tribe!
Wi' your pros and your cons wad ye decide
Gainst the 'sponsible voice o' a hale country-side
   On the facts 'bout Aiken-drum?

Though the "Brownie o' Blednoch" lang be gane,
The mark o' his feet's left on mony a stane;
And mony a wife and mony a wean
   Tell the feats o' Aiken-drum.

E'en now light loons that jibe and sneer
At spiritual guests and a' sic gear
At the Glashnock mill ha'e swat wi' fear
   And looked round for Aiken-drum.

And guidly folk ha'e gotten a fright
When the moon was set and the stars gied nae light
At the roaring linn in the howe o' the night
   Wi' sughs like Aiken-drum.

NOTES

1. In Nithsdale the Brownie wore a brown mantle and hood.
2. Galloway must have been alive with supernatural beings. M. M. Harper (*Rambles in Galloway*) lists a few of them: warlocks, witches, ghosts, worricows, kelpies, spunkies, carlines, fairies, brownies. There were also bogles, goblins and giants. The worricow was a hobgoblin—"Cow is a kind of de'il, but worricow is a worrying de'il." An old Gallovidian rhyme describes one that "sat on an auld grey stane and gaunted out 'Hech-how-hum'".
3. Harper has a local legend of a Brownie who undertook to hucht a farmer's sheep, and penned a few hares along with them, observing "Confoond thae wee grey anes! They cost me mair trouble than a' the lave o' them."
4. A communion cup belonging to John Macmillan, minister of Balmaghie, and used as a test of orthodoxy. Anyone who showed signs of agitation on picking it up was immediately suspect.

D

The Brownie and the Cannie Wife

Place: Nithsdale.
Source: R. H. Cromek, *Remains of Galloway and Nithsdale Song.*
Collector: Allan Cunningham.

A Brownie lived with Maxwell the Laird of Dalswinton, doing ten men's work and keeping the servants awake at nights with the noisy dirling of his flail. The Laird's daughter was the smallest lady in all the holms of Nithsdale and the Brownie was much attached to her, conveying her from her high-tower-chamber to the trysting thorn in the woods and back again with such light-heeled celerity that neither bird, dog nor servant awoke. He undressed her for the matrimonial bed and served her so hand-maiden-like that her attendant had nothing to do.

When the pains of childbirth seized her, a servant was sent for the cannie wife who lived across the Nith. The night was dark and the wind high and the servant loitered. The Brownie wrapped himself in his lady's fur cloak and rode through the flooded Nith. Mounting the old woman behind him he took the deep water back again.

"Ride nae by the auld pool," quo' she, "lest we meet wi' Brownie."

"Fear na, dame," quo' he, "ye've met wi' a' the Brownies ye'll meet."

Setting her down by the hall door, he hastened to the stables, where he found the servant lad just pulling on his boots and gave him a sound drubbing with his bridle.

At last a cleric, more zealous than wise, got the Laird's un-willing consent to have Brownie baptised. Concealing himself in the barn he waited until the little, wrinkled, ancient man appeared to begin his night's toil, then he leapt out and dashed the bap-tismal water in his face, repeating the words of the rite. The Brownie gave a frightful and agonising yell and vanished, never to return.

The Brownie of Cash

Place: Fife.
Source: *County Folklore* (Fife).

A Brownie who lived in the Castle of Cash used daily to cross the Meglo to the tower of Cash by stepping-stones. Here he used to labour cheerfully in the barn and in the byre, threshing the corn and milking the cows for the poor neighbours of the baron. Brownie was never visible to mortal, but his labour was daily observed, and all that he required in return was that he might be allowed to feed out of any dish he thought proper, though it had not been specially set apart for him.

One morning after a heavy rain the river was flooded and the stepping stones covered, so that the servants of Cash remarked to one another that Brownie would not be with them that day as there was no bridge nearer than that at the west end of the town, a considerable distance away. Just then, one of the maids who had taken the first spoonful from her cogful of porridge found the contents of the dish making a speedy disappearance—Brownie had been more anxious to serve her master than she had supposed.

When questioned as to how he had got over the water Brownie explained that he had "gone roun' by the brig"—hence the local proverb, "Gae roun' by the brig as Brownie did."

The Doonie

Place: Dumfriesshire.
Source: R. De B. Trotter, "Galloway Superstitions", *Gallovidian Annual*, vol. 5, 1903.

I mind my faither tellin' me that when he was a laddie at the skule ae afternoon him and some ithers gaed tae Crichope Linn lookin' for young doos, for there was a hantle o' them biggit there.

Ye ken what a queer bit Crichope is; juist like a muckle crack in the freestane rock, a' thrawn and crookit, wi' bits o' shelfs here an' there, an' holes that the doos biggit in; an' a' smooth't wi' the water that was rinnin' at the bottom, maybe thirty or forty feet doon.

Weel, he was thrang herryin' a nest an' pittin' the young doos in his jacket pooch, when his fit slippit and ow'er he gaed; an' juist as he was gaun oot o' sicht he gat a grip o' a hazel buss an' held on. He tried a' he could tae warsel up but he couldna, and it wasna lang or he fun' he couldna hang on muckle langer; an' he was lookin' doon tae see if he was gaun tae fa' on tae a craig an' get kill't or intae a pule an' get droon't, when he saw a queer lookin' aul' wife stannin' on a shelf near the bottom. She held oot her brat wi' baith haun's an' cry't oot, "Let gae an' A'll kep ye."

He didna think there was muckle chance o' her keppin' him, but he had tae let gae onyway, an' doon he fell on tae the aul' wife's apron. The apron didna kep him, for he skeytit aff it an' intae a deep pule, but the minute he cam' tae the tap the aul' wife gruppit him by the cuff o' the neck an' hailt him oot on the stanes, no a bit the waur.

He couldna think hoo she got there or hoo they were to wun oot, for the linn's a bit naebody can wun either oot or in o'; but she took him by the haun' and said, "C'wa this wey"; an' she led him oot by a wey he kent naethin' aboot an' could never fin' after, though he socht for't aften. And then she said, "Noo, scrieve for hame, an' dinna ye come here herryin' doos again, or maybe the Doonie'll no be here tae kep ye." An' when he turn't roon tae answer her she wisna there.

III

WITCHES, WARLOCKS AND THE DEVIL

WITCHES

EVERY parish in Scotland has its store of witch literature, varying from the hair-raising and curious to the dull or ludicrous, but capable now and then of a marvellous image:

> She has ta'en a small horn
> And loud and shrill blew she . . .

or, even more evocative,

> She's gathered witch dew in the Kells kirkyard
> In the mirk howe o' the moon . . .

Crazy or malevolent as most of them must have been, the witches have at least raised word magic. It sounds again as the coven "sits in the coat-tails of the moon" crying their greeting to the western star; and yet again in an eerie gathering song:

> When the grey howlet has three times hoo'd
> When the grimy cat has three times mew'd,
> When the Tod has yowled three times i' the wode
> At the red moon cowerin' ahin' the clud . . .
> Up horses a' . . .

Even the gruesome list of ingredients chawed together at the baking of a witch cake opens with a ballad ring:

> I saw yestreen, I saw yestreen,
> Little wis ye what I saw yestreen . . .

These fragments have their fascination but, to quote John Buchan, they "cast a queer crooked shadow from outer darkness"—a darkness which once overcast all Scotland, affecting life at every level, deep-rooted in the primitive belief in an all-pervasive and active evil principle. "Witchcraft," writes Cromek, "being no inheritance of the blood but the immediate gift of the devil, has been, by his artifice, always bestowed on those who could make most judicious use of it, for the annoyance of the righteous and the furtherance of perdition."[1]

The witch's power of terrorising a community often brought her a comfortable living, to the material as well as the spiritual annoyance of the righteous:

> Kimmer gets meat and kimmer gets meal,
> And cantie lives kimmer, right couthie and hale;
> Kimmer gets bread an' kimmer gets cheese,
> An' kimmer's uncanny e'en keep her at ease.

Houses planted about with rowan, elm, holly and yew had a certain amount of immunity from the devil's followers and Joseph Train has recorded the Galloway custom of fixing strips of bull's hide round the doors, windows and wall-heads of newly built houses, no evil spirit being able to approach a bull with even one white hair in his skin. Train also came across "an occult mixture of Rowan-tree twigs, with scraps of cloth and texts of scriptures bound up in part of a cow's hide", hidden in the rafters of a byre in the parish of Minnygaff. He asked some searching questions and discovered that a notorious witch had once lived hard by. Train handed on this find to Sir Walter Scott and it can be seen still in the museum at Abbotsford. It was also considered useful to carry about an iron ring, since a witch, working incognito, could be recognised by anyone looking through it.

After centuries of hidden growth, the sin of witchcraft came to the surface in the mid-sixteenth century when it appeared on the statute books of the Scottish Criminal Court. By an Act of 1563, Parliament made it illegal for any "manner of persoun or persounes of quhatsomever estate, degre or conditioun they be" to practise the black arts; but in spite of punishments as primitive as itself, the cult continued to flourish.

Occasionally it had its uses. When certain Armada ships, having escaped Howard and Drake, appeared on the Clyde it was the famous witch of Carrick, Eleine de Aggart, who wrought their destruction with a ball of blue yarn and secret spells. Nor was the Kirk itself above accepting discreet help. In 1697, apparently on the principle of setting a thief to catch a thief, the Kirk-Session of Stoneykirk hired a wise woman from Ayr to "discern" those in the parish who dealt in familiar spirits. Installed in the kirk itself, with the session clerk at her elbow, she scrutinised the entire community as it filed past, and the names of suspects were duly noted—the signal to write being a kick on the session clerk's ankle. The parish register was thereafter known as the Red Book of Stoneykirk and almost at once a phenomenal series of disasters began to strike the ministers who kept it, ceasing only when the book was publicly burned.

The last attempt to invoke the 1563 law against witchcraft is noted by Scott in the *Letters on Demonology and Witchcraft*. It took place in 1800 and ended unspectacularly in a sheriff's warning to the accused to control her tongue—an anti-climax which she seemed to find as vexing as her accuser did.

A lesser breed of witches lingered on, busy with such harmless ploys as the distilling of love potions. The remaining snatches of their cantrip rhymes have a kind of innocent gaiety and are worth remembering for the old botanical names preserved in them:

> Bourtree branches, yellow gowans,
> Berry rasps and berry rowans,
> De'il's milk frae thrissels saft,
> Clover leaves frae aff the craft,
> Binwud leaves, and blinman's baws,
> Heather bells and withered haws . . .
> Something sweet and something soor,
> Turn aboot wi' mild and dour;
> Hainie suckles, bluidy fingers,
> Napple roots and nettle stingers;
> Mix, mix, six and six,
> And the Auld Maid's cantrip fix.[2]

WARLOCKS

"Play us up 'Weel hoddled, Lucky.' Now this was a tune my gudesire learned frae a warlock that heard it when they were worshipping Satan at their meetings. My gudesire had sometimes played it at the ranting suppers at Redgauntlet Castle, but never very willingly, and now he grew cauld at the very name of it."[3]

Fiction admittedly, but an eerily exact reflection of that mixture of credulity, dread and curiosity evoked by Satan's followers in the old Scotland.

Not that all those branded as warlocks deserved the name, least of all that pathetic old man of Nithsdale who spent his life in voluntary exile rather than expose the community to the hazard of his uncanny eye. He was probably unique, but a good proportion of so-called wizards may well have been scholars, born in advance of their times.

Outstanding among these is Michael Scot.[4] Born about 1180 and regarded as unchancy in his native land, he was recognised in the Continental Schools as "the most illustrious doctor, Master Michael Scot, who amongst scholars is known as the supreme master". Apart from his post as tutor to the young Frederick II, afterwards Emperor, he studied mathematics and astronomy in Paris and distinguished himself among the Moorish scholars in Spain who were breaking new ground in chemistry, then called alchemy. A treatise on algebra, attributed to him and certainly contemporary, shows formulae and diagrams which must powerfully have suggested the black arts to the peasants and uneducated Border lairds among whom he is said to have ended his days.[5] Some two hundred years later the inventions of Napier of Merchiston, "Logarithms John", earned the same stigma. The tradition, still lingering round Edinburgh in the early nineteenth century, that his familiar spirit was a jet-black cock is interesting in view of the family's hereditary office of *pultriae regis*—king's poulterer.

If the breed of warlock emerges with a touch of dignity lacking among witches, this may be due to the leavening of genuine scholarship in their ranks.

THE DEVIL

"What was he like?" the eager neighbours demanded of a man who claimed to have met the devil and the answer was that apart from a terrible head of horns, long hairy legs, great cloven feet and a smell of brimstone, he had seemed "a gey decent-like chiel".

A very old jibe, probably of French origin, declares that when Satan was displaying the kingdoms of this world and all the glory of them he very prudently "keipit his muckle thoom on Scotland". His reason, of course, was to hide the extreme poverty of the land, but it is possible that he also foresaw the unique relationship awaiting him with the Scottish people, and their tendency, however disapprovingly, to give him his due.

The popular tales reflect this reluctant tolerance, crediting the devil with a liking for such pleasant and innocent things as the smell of newly sawn wood and the early morning air; and there is the engaging pre-Reformation tradition that, rather than be horn idle on Fridays when the Church took over his usual clientele, he kept open house for any goat who might care to have its beard trimmed on that day. Hence the popular taunt thrown at truants—"had this been Friday I could hae sworn ye had been awa' wi' the gates at the De'il getting your beard redd!"[6]

But a genuine and far from humorous belief in the devil had a grip on the nation. Most parishes had their "feart places", untouched by the plough, overgrown by nettles and briars, propitiatingly known as the Gudeman's croft;[7] and terror was sharpened by the conviction that the evil principle went about in disguise, taking the shape of a black dog, a brindled cat, a goat, a horse, a black ram. This enhanced his power, but there were certain restrictions. The body of a drake could be appropriated, but cocks and hens were too quick for the devil while the pigeon, having no gall bladder, was not a suitable medium. For obvious reasons a lamb was inviolable and the choice of human shapes was limited by his own vanity. Satan fancied himself as a tall gentleman, well-groomed, well-spoken and fatally attractive to the unwary, whom he tried to entangle with subtle questions. Sometimes his presence was announced by "a loud and goustie wind that tirled the rafters and gar'd the divots stoor aff the riggin'."[8]

Only silver bullets could harm him, and the protective quality of this metal was such that a man with one silver coin in his pocket might say: "I hae gotten as muckle siller as keep the de'il aff me, and nae mair."

NOTES

1. The land was literally witch-ridden. One small Border hamlet boasted a round dozen at one time—five of them inhabiting the "Kirk Row". Protective measures against them were considered as necessary as burglar precautions are now.

2. Mactaggart's *Scottish Gallovidian Encyclopedia*.

3. See "Wandering Willie's Tale", from *Redgauntlet*.

4. See *The Life and Legend of Michael Scot*, The Rev. J. Wood Brown. Edinburgh, 1897.

5. Cf. Clarke's "Three Laws"—(3) "any sufficiently advanced technology is indistinguishable from magic". *Report on Planet 3*, 1972.

6. Joseph Train. See p. 139. "Some Collectors of the Tales."

7. "A piece of ground never touched by plough or spade, a dismal breadth of land set aside for the evil one." *County Folklore* (Fife).

8. *Transactions of the Hawick Archeological Society*.

The Witches' Tryst[1]

Place: Nithsdale.
Source: R. H. Cromek, *Remains of Galloway and Nithsdale Song.*
Narrator: "An old man of Caerlaverock."
Collector: Allan Cunningham.

I gaed out ae fine simmer night to haud my halve at the Pow fit. It was twal' o clock, an' a' was lowne; the moon had just gotten up—ye might a' gathered preens! I heard something firsle like silk—I glowered roun, an' what saw I but a bonnie boat, wi' a nob o' gowd, an' sails like new-coincd siller. It was only but a wee bittie frae me, I might amaist touch't it.

"Gude speed ye, gif ye gan for guid," quo' I, for I dreed our auld Carlin was casting some o' her pranks.

Another cunning boat cam' aff Caerla'rick to meet it. Thae twa bade a stricken hour thegither sidie for sidie.

"Haith," quo' I, "the deil's grit wi' some!" Sae I crap doon amang some lang cowes till Luckie cam' back.

The boat played bowte agin' the bank, an' out lowpes Kimmer, wi' a pyked naig's head i' her han'.

"Lord be about us!" quo' I, for she cam straught for me. She howked up a green turf, covered her bane, an' gaed her wa's.

When I thought her hame, up I gat and pu'd up the bane an' hid it. I was fley'd to gae back for twa or three nights, lest the deil's minnie should wyte me for her uncannie boat, an' lair me 'mang the sludge, or may be do waur. I gaed back howsever; an' on that night o' the moon wha comes to me but Kimmer!

"Rabbin," quo' she, "fand ye ane auld bane amang the cowes?"

"Deed no, it may be gowd for me!" quo' I.

"Weel, weel," quo' she, "I'll byde an' help ye hamc wi' your fish." God's be my help, naught grippit I but tades an' paddocks!

"Satan, thy nieve's here," quo' I. "Ken ye" (quo' I) o' yon' new cheese our wyf took but frae the chessel yestreen? I'm gaun to send't t'ye the morning, yere a gude neebor to me:—an' heer'st thou me! there's a bit auld bane whomeled aneath thae cowes; I kent nae it was thine."

Kimmer drew't out; "Aye, aye, its my auld bane; weel speed ye!"

I' the very first pow I gat sic a louthe o' fish that I carried till my back cracked again.

NOTE

1. Caerlaverock and New Abbey each had a famous witch. The pair used to meet on the night of every full moon "to devise employment for the coming month", but after the Kirk had forbidden all such meetings on land they fixed their trysts on the water between the two parishes.

The Witch of Deloraine

Place: Borders.
Source: Thomas Wilkie, *Old Rites, Ceremonies and Customs of the Inhabitants of the Southern Counties of Scotland.*

The farmer's wife of Deloraine engaged the tailors to work at her house. They started early, and when breakfast time came she brought them porridge and milk. One of the apprentices noticed that when the milk was nearly finished the gudewife slipped out to the door with the basin in her hand. He followed and watched her turn a pin in the wall, whereupon a stream of milk poured into the basin. When she turned the pin again the stream of milk stopped. The basin was then set down by the tailors, who finished their porridge with it.

At noon the workers began to get thirsty and the apprentice offered to get them a drink of milk. Making sure that the gudewife was not about, he turned the pin in the wall and out poured the milk into his basin. But when he turned it back again the milk still ran.

He called his friends and they hurried to get every tub and jug and empty vessel in the house, but the milk filled them all and still it poured.

At last the gudewife came back and when she saw what had happened she cried out in a fiendish voice: "A' ye loons, ye hae drawn a' the milk frae every cow between the head o' Yarrow and the foot o't. This day ne'er a cow will gie a drap o' milk to its

master, although he were going to starve."[1]

Hence, to this day, the wives of Deloraine will never feed tailors on onything but champit tatties[2] and cabbage.[3]

NOTES

1. This theft of milk from a cow was called "airt magic", the belief being that the milk could be drawn from as far off as a bull could be heard to roar. "We plait the rope the wrong way in the devil's name."

2. A Stewartry woman of last century had a special way with champit tatties. They were "scraped, well dried, boiled, salted, beetled, buttered, milked and rumbled"—and never forgotten by anyone fortunate enough to taste them.

3. Some indication of the dishes traditional to certain occasions can be gleaned from the Tales.

   The curlers' dinner was beef and greens; swinglers of the lint—those who beat the flax—got champit tatties and butter with whey and lappered milk; at a Border Kirn there would be haggis, flesh and kail, singed sheep's head, tatties "dressed baith ways" (roasted and boiled), dumplings with greens, and a whang o' the gudewife's cheese. Hallowe'en supper was usually sowens and butter; Fastern's E'en, ushering in Lent, was celebrated with cockaleeky. At a birth tea and cheese were provided, often with shortbread to follow, and in Galloway the custom was for neighbours to call with a birth offering of eggs, cheese, a print of butter and perhaps a braxy ham.

The Witch of Kirkhope

Place: Selkirkshire.
Source: James Hogg, *The Queen's Wake* (Notes).

A number of gentlemen were one day met for a chase on the lands of Newhouse and Kirkhope. Their greyhounds were many and keen, but not a hare did they raise.

At last a boy came to them offering to start a hare if they would give him a guinea and the black greyhound to hold. The demand was singular, but it was peremptory and on no other condition would he comply; so the guerdon was paid.

A hare was started at once and the sport was excellent, but the greyhounds were baffled. One by one they were beginning to give up the chase when one of the party came slyly behind the boy and cut the leash in which he was holding the black dog.

Away flew the dog to join the chase while the boy ran, bawling out with great vociferation: "Hey, mither, rin! Hey, ye auld witch, rin if ever ye ran i' your life! Rin, mither, rin!'

The black dog came fast up with the hare and was just beginning to mouth her when she sprang in at a cottage window and escaped. When the riders entered the cottage they found no hare, or any living creature but an old woman lying panting on the bed, so breathless that she could not speak a word.

The Witch of Kirkcowan

Place: Dumfriesshire.
Source: R. C. Reid, "Traditions of Kirkcowan."
Narrator: "Mr. McWilliam of Kirkcowan" (b. 1825).
   This is a variation on Hogg's tale, but the occupation of hare-hunter seldom appears in the records.

Nanny McMillan was a witch. Even stout-hearted folk hurried past her cottage in the gloaming and always treated her with respect. She lived just outside the manse gate.

There was also in Kirkcowan a hare hunter, who had remarkable skill in bringing down the swiftest hare. He plied his trade, a profitable one in those days, around the village and particularly on a part of the glebe behind the manse which runs down to the river, where the broom and whins gave shelter to the hares. He was also most skilled in tracking wounded hares.

There was one parti-coloured hare, large and fine, which he saw often but never could secure. Bullets seemed not to touch it. Day after day he watched it at play on the glebe land, day after day it defied all his efforts and craft. At last he put a silver bullet in his pocket, knowing this to be infallible against witchcraft and fairy wiles.

When his chance came to shoot, the hare rolled head over heels into the whins, then suddenly recovered and made for the village, the hare-hunter after it. He could see its head bleeding and knew where he had wounded it.

At Nanny McMillan's cottage it ran round an angle of the wall and was lost. In spite of all his tracking skill the hare hunter could find no traces beyond that point. Summoning up his courage he knocked at Nanny's door. At first there was no answer, but repeated knocking produced a request to wait a moment. At last the door opened a chink and an agitated voice asked what he wanted.

Had she seen a parti-coloured hare pass the door? No. She had seen nothing.

"Are ye sure?" urged the man, pushing into the doorway in

his eagerness. Then he retreated, for there stood old Nanny, her head bound up just above the eye where his silver bullet had struck the uncanny beast.

Maggie Osborne

Place: Ayrshire.
Source: William Robertson, *Historical Tales of Ayrshire*.

Maggie Osborne of Ayr was a witch of strong character. A natural daughter of the Warlock Laird of Fail, she had been carefully instructed in the black arts by her father and so many devils attended her midnight excursions into Galloway that no grass grows to this day on her path over the Carrick hills—still known as "Maggie's gate to Galloway".

One evening as she was passing over the Nick of the Balloch she saw a large funeral approach and as some of the mourners had good cause to know her she changed herself into the form of a beetle and was creeping along the side of the road when one of the men unwittingly set his foot on her. Being in a hollow, she was saved, but from that time she strove with all her arts to ruin the man. Success did not come until one evening when he forgot to say grace before supper. His good angel promptly deserted him. Maggie rolled a wreath of snow on his house and killed the whole family except one son who was visiting friends in the Hebrides.

But even he was not to escape. When his ship reached the Bay of Ayr Maggie shut herself in the garret telling her maid to fill a mash tun with water, set an ale-cap floating, and await further orders.

Three times the maid was sent to report on how things went with the bicker. The first time it was rocking on rippling water; the second time the water was rising over the lip of the tun, dashing the bicker from side to side; the third time there was calm water and the bicker had disappeared.

"The de'il has served me weel for ance," said Maggie, and news soon came that the ship had been dashed in pieces on Nicholas Rock at the Bar of Ayr.

On another occasion she quarrelled with her maid and forced her to brew by night. About midnight some cats leaped into the brew house and began to fight. One sprang suddenly on the girl and tried to push her into a cooler filled with boiling worts, but she snatched a ladle and scalded the cat instead. Next morning Maggie was found with a blistered back.

She was finally tried for witchcraft and sentenced to be burned, her last remark being addressed to the devil: "Oh ye fause loon, instead o' a black gown ye hae gi'en me a red ane; hae I deserved this for serving ye sae lang?"

E

Witch and Warlock

Place: Borders.
Source: James Hogg, *The Queen's Wake.*

Hogg, who used to boast of several witches in his own ancestry, says: "The best old witch story that remains is that which is related of the celebrated Michael Scot, Master of Oakwood. The old people tell it as follows (the narrator would almost certainly be his mother):

There was one of Maister Michael's tenants who had a wife that was the most notable witch of her age. So extraordinary were her powers that the country people began to say that in some cantrips she surpassed the Master. Michael could ill brook such insinuations, for there is much jealousy between such characters, and one day he went over with his dogs in pretence of hunting, but really intent on chastisement.

He found the woman alone in the field weeding lint and asked her in a friendly manner to show him some of her powerful art. She was angry, and denied that she had any supernatural skill. He pressed her, and was sharply told to leave her alone or he would have reason to repent.

Then she snatched the wand from his hand and gave him three sharp lashes with it. Instantly he was changed to a hare.[1]

"Shu, Michael! Rin or dee!" she cried, laughing, and baited his own dogs on him.

He was hard hunted and had to swim the river and take shelter in the sewer of his own castle, where he changed himself again to the shape of a man.

Furious at being outwitted, Michael planned his revenge. He sent his man to Fauldshope, where the witch lived, to borrow bread for his dogs. If she gave him the bread he was to thank her and come away; but if she refused it he was to lodge above the lintel of her door a line written in red characters.

The servant found the wife of Fauldshope baking bread, as Michael had assured him he would. She received him ungraciously and refused to give him bread, alleging that she had not enough to feed her own reapers. The man lodged the line over the lintel and returned to his Master.

The spell began at once to work. Throwing off her clothes, the woman took to dancing round and round the fire, singing:

> Master Michael Scot's man
> Cam seekin' bread and gat nane.

At midday the reapers looked in vain for the gudewife bringing their dinner. The gudeman sent a servant lassie off to help her, but she failed to return. At length, suspecting that his wife had taken some of her tiravees, he sent the reapers home. Every one of them went into the farmhouse, and as soon as each passed under the lintel he was seized with the mania. The gudeman had stopped to get some ears of corn, and hearing the din when he reached the house he looked in at the window. There were all his people, dancing naked round the fire singing with the most frantic wildness,

> Master Michael Scot's man
> Cam seekin' bread and gat nane.

His wife, half exhausted, was being trailed round. She could only utter an occasional syllable of the song in a kind of scream; but she was as intent on the sport as ever.

The gudeman mounted his horse and rode with all speed to the Master, asking why he had put all his people mad. Michael bade him take down the note from the lintel and burn it, and as soon as this was done the people returned to their senses.

But the gudewife died overnight, leaving Michael unmatched and alone in the arts of enchantment and necromancy.[2]

NOTES

1. "Glamour, in the legends of Scottish superstition, means the magic power of imposing on the eyesight of spectators so that the appearance of an object shall be wholly different from the reality. The transformation of Michael Scot by the witch of Fauldshope was the genuine operation of glamour." Scott, *Lay of the Last Minstrel*, note xxxi.
2. This death dance was one of the spells cast on animals. A farmer complained that his "pickle sheep have a' been bewitched, and a great part o' them have died dancing hornpipes and French cortillions".

Michael Scot's Journey to Rome

Place: West of Scotland.
Source: Lord Archibald Campbell, *Waifs and Strays of Celtic Tradition*, vol. I.

This tale has much in common with the tales of German sorcerers. Faust called up three spirits, the first as swift as an arrow, the second as the wind, the third as the thought of man.

When Scotland was ruled by the Pope the people were very ignorant, and nothing could be done without the Pope's consent. The Feast of Shrove-tide regulated all the feasts of the year, so when the date of Shrove-tide was known the date of every other feast in the year was also known. Every year an intelligent, clever, fearless, prudent and well-bred man was selected to go to Rome and ascertain the date of Shrove-tide, and on a certain year Michael Scot, a learned man and famous, was chosen; but because of many other matters he forgot his duty until Candlemas. There was not a minute to lose.

He took himself to one of the fairy riding fillies, and said: "How swift are you?"

"I am as fleet as the wind."

"You will not do," says Michael.

He reached the second one: "How swift are you?"

"I am so swift that I can outspeed the wind that comes behind me, and overtake the wind that goes before me."

"You will not do," answered Michael.

The third one was as fleet as the black blast of March.

"Scarcely will you do," said Michael, and put the question to the fourth.

"I am as swift as the thought of a maiden between her two lovers."

"You will be of service," says Michael. "Make ready."

"I am always ready if the man were in accord with me," says she.

They started. Sea and land were alike to them. While they were above the sea the witch said to him: "What say the women of Scotland when they quench the fire?"

"You ride," says Michael , "in your master's name, and never mind that."

"Blessing to thyself but a curse on thy teacher," replied she.

"What," says she again, "say the wives of Scotland when they put the first weanling to bed?"

"Ride you in your master's name and let the wives of Scotland sleep," responded Michael.

"Forward was the woman who put the first finger in your mouth," says she.

Michael arrived at Rome. It was morning. He sent swift word to the Pope that the messenger from Scotland was at the door seeking knowledge of Shrove-tide, lest Lent would go away. The Pope came at once to the audience room.

"Whence art thou?" he said to Michael.

"I am from thy faithful children in Scotland, seeking the knowledge of Shrove-tide, lest Lent will go away."

"You were too late in coming."

"Early that leases me," replied Michael.

"You have ridden somewhat high."

"Neither high nor low but right ahead," says Michael.

"I see," says the Pope, "snow on your bonnet."

"Yes, by your leave, the snow of Scotland."

"What proof," says the Pope, "can you give me of that? Likewise that you have come from Scotland to seek knowledge of Shrove-tide?"

"That," says Michael, "shoe on your foot is not your own."

The Pope looked, and on his right foot was a woman's shoe.

"You will get what you want," says he to Michael, "and begone. The first Tuesday of the first moon of spring is Shrove-tide."

Thus Michael Scot obtained knowledge of the secret that the Pope kept to himself.

The Devil in Search of a Trade

Place: Borders.
Source: Thomas Wilkie, "Old Rites, Ceremonies and Customs of the Inhabitants of the Southern Counties of Scotland."

The Devil wanted to learn a trade.

First he went to a weaver, but when he pricked his finger with the hanks of the Temples he disowned that occupation.

As apprentice to a tailor he sewed his finger to the cloth and spoiled the sleeve of a coat he was making for a gentleman, so his master, in a passion, knocked him over the board with the goose;[1] so he went to a blacksmith who set him to shoe a horse. He pricked the horse and drove the nail into his own finger, and when he tried to make a shoe the chaper[2] struck the mouth of the tongs and so pinched him that he left the smithy.

After that he went to a ferrier who ordered him to cauterise a horse, but he heated the iron too hot which so enraged his master that he swore he would rump him and pare his nails if he did not leave at once; so he became a travelling tinker. Here he made his rivets so fast that he split the cauldrons and tore the bellows, and his master was glad to get quit of him.

Next he betook himself to the occupation of a carpenter at which he wounded himself with the axe, bruised himself with the plane, and took so many tumbles from the upper side of the logs he had to saw that he decided to quit, though with the greatest eluctance as he was delighted by the smell of new wood and the charming morning and evening walks with his fellow apprentices to and from their work.

The job of shoemaker greatly enamoured him till his master gave him a severe yerkin' with the foot-stirrup for taking the wrong measure of a lady's foot and not being able to tell the number of substicks necessary to finish a pair of shoes after he had been in the business three months. This induced him to make a rive in the upper leather of his indenture and take his leave.

He next became a musician[3] and poet and strolled the country singing songs of his own composing which were much esteemed by free thinkers. In the evening he frequented low ale-houses where he played the pipes.

Finally he became a soldier and led a band of infernal rascals until they were all confined in the bottomless pit.[4]

NOTES

1. Knocked him off the table with the tailor's iron.
2. This should probably read "chapper". The chapper was the black-smith's assistant, the man who wielded the sledge-hammer. (He was also

called the fore-hammerman.) The devil would be holding the molten horseshoe in the tongs and the nasty accident resulting from a misdirected blow from the chapper can be easily visualised.

3. Another glimpse of the devil as musician is provided by the Hawick Archeological Society in its transactions: "Oh! sic a sicht! The de'il was sitting in an auld elbow chair and aboot hauf a score o' witches aroond and the gudewife at his right hand. The company partook of wine and apples, except for the auld ane himsel', who got the bagpipes out and set them a' dancing." This in the decent Teviotside village of Allanhaugh.

4. But he may have found his vocation in the end: witness the adage once current in Edinburgh, "Hame's hame, as the de'il said when he took a seat in the Court of Session".

The Fause Knight

Place: Galloway.
Source: Motherwell, *Minstrelsy Ancient and Modern.*
Collector: William Motherwell.

"A nursery tale of Galloway, and a specimen of a class of composition of great antiquity representing the Enemy of Mankind in the endeavour to confound a mortal with questions."

"O where are ye gaun?"
    Quo' the fause knight upon the road;
"I'm gaun to the scule,"
    Quo' the wee boy, and still he stude.

"What is that upon your back?"
    Quo' the fause knight upon the road;
"Atweel it's my bukes,"[1]
    Quo' the wee boy, and still he stude.

"What's that ye've got in your arm?"
    Quo' the fause knight upon the road;
"Atweel it's my pcit,"[2]
    Quo' the wee boy, and still he stude.

"Wha's aucht thae sheep?"
    Quo' the fause knight upon the road;
"They're mine and my mother's,"
    Quo' the wee boy, and still he stude.

"How mony o' them are mine?"
　Quo' the fause knight upon the road;
"A' they that hae blue tails,"
　Quo' the wee boy, and still he stude.

"I wiss ye were on yon tree,"
　Quo' the fause knight upon the road;
"And a guid ladder under me,"
　Quo' the wee boy, and still he stude.

"And the ladder for to break,"
　Quo' the fause knight upon the road,
"And you for to fa' down,"
　Quo' the wee boy, and still he stude.

"I wiss ye were in yon sie,"
　Quo' the fause knight upon the road;
"And a guid bottom under me,"
　Quo' the wee boy, and still he stude.

"And the bottom for to break,"
　Quo' the fause knight upon the road;
"*And ye to be drowned,*"
　Quo' the wee boy, and still he stude.

NOTES

1. The chief book used in school might be the Bible. "Once through the Bible" was considered a fair education in many dame-schools of the eighteenth century. One such, in the parish of Kirkpatrick-Durham, was attended by Allan Cunningham's younger brother. The Dame, Nancy Kingan, taught the alphabet, the Shorter Catechism, the Psalms of David and the Proverbs of Solomon. Spelling she considered a waste of time. She did not pretend to writing or arithmetic and had never heard of grammar, but her boast was that "the bairns when they lea' ma schule hae unco little to learn o' the Bible".

　　Inspired teachers, of course, far outnumbered the oddities. Carlyle's father, born in 1758 and "never more than three months at any school", emerged from his brief contact with education having acquired "a solid knowledge of Arithmetic, a fine antique Handwriting".

2. "Peit"—the peat carried by the scholar for the master's fire.

IV

THE UNIVERSAL THEMES

I T was the Reverend Mr. Balwhidder who complained that between the booming of the muckle wheel and the birring of the little wheel under the vigorous direction of his second wife, the manse of Dalmailing was like an organ kist.[1] At the time his simile would have covered the whole of Scotland. "The big wheel and the little wheel were birring in every parlour and kitchen, throwing off abundance of woollen and linen yarn. Home made clothing had infinitely more bield and durability than the fine (manufactured) broadcloth, and what webs of linen used to be seen spread out to bleach!"[2] With every farmer growing and dressing[3] his own flax and every self-respecting housewife spinning her own web (two hanks a day, according to a journal of 1692) the country must literally have vibrated to the rhythms of spinning and weaving.

It was against these rhythms that the Tales were first evolved. The measured throb of spinning wheels, continuous since the beginning of civilisation, must have helped to draw out the universal story themes from the tangled dreams and perplexities of the race mind, as the distaff drew out the thread. These themes—name-guessing, bespelled brides and bridegrooms, supernatural helpers, enchanted journeys, impossible tasks—mark the genuine fairy story, setting it in a timeless context apart from tales and legends of supernatural beings which can be pinned to a calendar and a map. The opening formula, "ance there was a man"—or an auld wife or a king's dochter—has as little bearing on clock-time as the "In the beginning" of Genesis. The Debateable Grund of Whuppity Stoorie has a double meaning, hinting at the land of Faerie where nothing, however apparently familiar, is to be taken at its face value.

So as the wheels thrummed in sixteenth and seventeenth century Scotland the old patterns were re-created in the Lowland idiom. The frog prince, long familiar in Germany, came loup-loup-louping from a well in Fife; Rumpelstiltskin—her face like the faur end o' a fiddle—mounted a Nithsdale brae; and Cinderella, first told in tenth-century China, reappeared in Ayrshire as "pure tynt Rashiecoat".[4]

And so it seems fitting to open a group of Scottish variations on the universal story themes with three tales built round the spinning wheel itself.

There are two main types of spinning tale, both involving an impossible task, a supernatural helper and the guessing of a name. This name-guessing motif is one of the oldest and most interesting threads in the fabric of folklore, running back to the primitive confusion between symbol and reality (cf. life-index motif in Celtic tales). Some hold that this confusion helped to shape the Roman law of property, so it may still be with us, lurking in the unlikely ambience of the Register of Sasines. The metaphysically inclined will find interesting ideas on the subject in a talk, *Kafka, Rilke and Rumpelstiltskin*, broadcast by Professor Idris Parry and published in *The Listener* of 2nd December 1965.

The Rev. William Gregor caught a whiff of this primitive thought in the reluctance of country folk in the early nineteenth century to give their names to a servant when calling at a town house. Perhaps it was still lingering in the mind of an old lady of the twentieth century who was not surprised to learn that astronomers could weigh and measure the stars. After all, that was what they were paid to do. But— "How did they manage to find out their *names*?"

NOTES

1. John Galt, *Annals of the Parish.*
2. James Russell, *Reminiscences of Yarrow.*
3. The flax stalks were gathered, soaked, spread out on lea-land to dry, beaten and finally heckled. In the early nineteenth century a quarter acre for flax growing was part of a cottager's allowance. *Recollections of a Roxburghshire Woman.*
4. *The Complaynt of Scotland.*

Whuppity Stoorie[1]

Place: Dumfriesshire.
Source: Robert Chambers, *Popular Rhymes of Scotland*.
Narrator: Charles Kirkpatrick Sharpe, from the exact words of
Nurse Jenny of Hoddam.

I ken ye're fond o' clashes aboot fairies, bairns; and a story anent
a fairy and the goodwife o' Kittlerumpit has joost come into my
mind; but I canna very weel tell ye noo whereaboots Kittlerumpit lies. I think it's somewhere in amang the Debateable
Grund; onygate I'se no pretend to mair than I ken.

But hoosoever, the goodman o' Kittlerumpit was a vaguing
sort o' a body; and he gaed to a fair ae day, and not only never
came hame again but never mair was heard o'. Some said he listed,
and ither some that the wearifu' press gang cleekit him up,
though he was clothed wi' a wife and a wean forbye. Hech-how!
that dulefu' press gang! they gaed aboot the kintra like roarin'
lions, seekin' whom they micht devoor. I mind weel, my auldest
brither Sandy was a' but smoored in the meal ark hiding frae thae
limmers. After they war gane we pu'd him oot frae amang the
meal, pechin' and greetin' and as white as ony corp. Ma mither
had to pike the meal oot o' his mooth wi' the shank o' a horn
spoon.

Aweel, when the goodman o' Kittlerumpit was gane, the goodwife was left wi' sma' fendin'. Little gear had she, and a sookin'
lad bairn. A'body said they war sorry for her; but naebody helpit
her, whilk's a common case, sirs. Howsomever, the goodwife
had a soo, and that was her only consolation; for the soo was soon
to farra, and she hopit for a good bairn-time.

But we a' weel ken hope's fallacious. Ae day the wife gaes to
the sty to fill the soo's trough; and what does she find but the soo
lying on her back, grunting and graning, and ready to gie up the
ghost.

I trow this was a new stoond to the goodwife's heart; sae she
sat doon on the knockin'-stane,[2] wi' her bairn on her knee, and
grat sairer than ever she did for the loss o' her ain goodman.

Noo, I premeese that the cot-hoose o' Kittlerumpit was biggit on a brae, wi' a muckle fir-wood behint it, o' whilk ye may hear or lang gae. So the goodwife, when she was dichtin' her e'en, chances to look down the brae, and what does she see but an auld woman, amaist like a leddy, coming slowly up the gaet. She was buskit in green, a' but a white short apron, and a black velvet hood, and a steeple-crowned beaver-hat on her head. She had a lang walking staff, as lang as hersel', in her hand—the sort of staff that auld men and auld women helpit themselves wi' lang syne; I see nae sic staffs noo, sirs.

Aweel, when the goodwife saw the green gentlewoman near her, she rase and made a curchie; and "Madam," quo' she, greetin', "I'm ane of the maist misfortunate women alive."

"I dinna wish to hear pipers' news and fiddlers' tales, goodwife," quo' the green woman. "I ken ye've tint your goodman—we had waur losses at the Shirra Muir; and I ken that your sow's unco sick. Noo, what will ye gie me gin I cure her?"

"Onything your leddyship's madam likes," quo' the witless goodwife, never guessin' wha she had to deal wi'.

"Let's wat thooms³ on that bargain," quo' the green woman: sae thooms were wat, I'se warrant ye; and into the sty madam marches.

She looks at the sow wi' a lang glower, and syne began to mutter to hersel' what the goodwife couldna weel understand; but she said it sounded like:

> Pitter patter,
> Haly water.

Syne she took oot o' her pooch a wee bottle, wi' something like oil in't, and rubs the soo wi't abune the snoot, ahint the lugs, and on the tip o' the tail. "Get up, beast," quo' the green woman. Nae sooner said nor done—up bangs the soo wi' a grunt, and awa' to the trough for her breakfast.

The goodwife o' Kittlerumpit was a joyfu' goodwife noo, and wad hae kissed the very hem o' the green madam's gown-tail, but she wadna let her. "I'm no sae fond o' fashions," quo' she; "but noo that I hae richted your sick beast, let us end our sicker bargain. You'll no find me an unreasonable greedy body—I aye like to do a good turn for a sma' reward—a' I ask, and *wull* hae, is that lad bairn in your bosom."

The goodwife o' Kittlerumpit, wha noo kent her customer, ga'e a skirl like a stickit gryse. The green woman was a fairy, nae doubt; sae she prays, and greets, and begs, and flytes; but a' wadna do. "Ye may spare your din," quo' the fairy, "skirling as if I was as deaf as a doornail; but this I'll let ye to wut—I canna, *by the law we leeve on*,[4] take your bairn till the third day after this day; and no then, if ye can tell me my right name." Sae madam gaes awa' round the swine's-sty end, and the good wife fa's doon in a swerf behint the knockin'-stane.

Aweel, the goodwife o' Kittlerumpit could sleep nane that nicht for greetin', an' a' the next day the same, cuddlin' her bairn till she near squeezed its breath out; but the second day she thinks o' takin' a walk in the wood I telt ye o'; and sae, wi' the bairn in her arms, she sets out, and gaes far in amang the trees, where was an old quarry hole grown owre wi' gerse, and a bonny spring well in the middle o't. Before she came very nigh she hears the birring o' a lint-wheel, and a voice lilting a sang; sae the wife creeps quietly amang the bushes, and keeks ower the broo o' the quarry, and what does she see but the green fairy kemping[5] at her wheel, and singing like ony precentor:

> Little kens our guid dame at hame[6]
> That Whuppity Stoorie is my name!

"Ah, ha!" thinks the wife, "I've gotten the mason's word at last; the deil gie them joy that tell't it!" Sae she gaed hame far lichter than she came out, as ye may weel guess, lauchin' like a madcap wi' the thought o' begunkin' the auld green fairy.

Aweel, ye maun ken that this goodwife was a jokus woman, and aye merry when her heart wasna unco sair owreladen. Sae she thinks to hae some sport wi' the fairy; and at the appointit time she puts the bairn behint the knockin'-stane, and sits down on't hersel'. Syne she pu's her mutch ajee owre her left lug, crooks her mou on the tither side, as gin she war greetin', and a filthy face she made, ye may be sure. She hadna lang to wait, for up the brae mounts the green fairy, nowther lame nor lazy; and lang or she gat near the knockin'-stane, she skirls out: "Goodwife o' Kittlerumpit, ye weel ken what I come for—stand and deliver!" The wife pretends to greet sairer than before, and wrings her nieves, and fa's on her knees wi': "Och, sweet madam mistress, spare my only bairn, and take the weary soo!"

"The deil take the soo for my share," quo' the fairy; "I come na here for swine's flesh. Dinna be contramawcious, hizzie, but gie me the gett instantly."

"Ochon, dear leddy mine," quo' the greetin' goodwife; "forbear my poor bairn and take mysel'!"

"The deil's in the daft jad," quo' the fairy, looking like the faur end o' a fiddle; "I'll wad she's clean dementit. Wha in a' the earthly warld, wi' half an ee in their head, wad ever meddle wi' the likes o' thee?"

I trow this set up the wife o' Kittlerumpit's birse; for though she had twa bleert een, and a lang red neb forbye, she thought hersel' as bonny as the best o' them. Sae she bangs aff her knees, sets up her mutch-croon, and wi' her twa hands faulded afore her, she maks a curchie down to the grund, and, "In troth, fair madam," quo' she, "I might hae had the wit to ken that the likes o' me is na fit to tie the warst shoe-strings o' the heich and mighty princess, *Whuppity Stoorie!*"

Gin a fluff o' gunpowder had come oot o' the grund, it couldna hae gart the fairy loup heicher nor she did; syne doon she came again, dump on her shoe-heels, and whurlin' round, she ran down the brae, scraichin' for rage, like a houlet chased wi' the witches.

The goodwife o' Kittlerumpit leugh till she was like to ryve; syne she tak's up her bairn, and gaes into her hoose singin' till't a' the gaet:

> A goo and a gitty, my bonny wee tyke,
> Ye'se noo hae your four-oories;
> Sin' we've gi'en Nick a bane to pyke,
> Wi' his wheels and his Whuppity Stoories.

NOTES

1. This tale belongs to the first type of spinning story in which the helper is out to strike a hard bargain and the plot turns on his (or her) defeat. The usual formula runs: Impossible task—supernatural help with bargain—secret name overheard—deliverance. Rumpelstiltskin is the prototype and variants of the tale have been found in Austria, France, Germany, Iceland, Italy, Russia, Spain and other parts of Britain; but the Scottish Whuppity Stoorie takes its independent way, replacing the impossible task with an impossible situation—a dying pig to be revived: in other words, the all too familiar poverty situation.

2. Knocking-stane—a stone mortar in which the husks were beaten off the barley with a wooden mallet.

3. i.e. seal the bargain by wetting thumbs. Anyone wishing to delve deeper should consult *The American Folklore Society Journal*, vol. 3, "Saliva Superstitions", F. D. Bergen.

4. This hints at the mysterious embargo restricting fairy machinations against mortals.

5. The aggressive fairy character in a word—she even *strives* with her spinning-wheel.

6. It is interesting that the name is always revealed in verse or song. See George Puttenham, *The Art of Poesy*: ". . . the American, the Perusine and the very Canniball, do sing and also say, their highest and holiest matters in certaine riming versicles and not in prose . . ."

Habetrot[1]

Place: Roxburghshire.
Source: Thomas Wilkie, "Old Rites, Ceremonies and Customs of the Southern Counties of Scotland."
Collector: Thomas Wilkie (c. 1820).

A Selkirkshire woman had one fair daughter who loved to play better than to work, and would be out in the fields instead of sitting at her distaff. As no lassie had the chance of a good husband unless she could spin, this vexed the woman sorely. She cajoled and threatened her daughter, but all to no purpose. The girl remained an idle cuttie.

At last, one spring morning, the gudewife brought out seven heads of lint, saying that they must be spun into yarn without fail in three days. Aware that her mother meant what she said, the lassie did her best, but by the evening of the second day only a very small part of the task was done. She cried herself to sleep, and in the morning, throwing aside her work in despair, ran out into the fields, all sparkling with dew.[2] Close by the burn she found a little knoll covered with flowers and there she flung herself down, hiding her face in her hands.

When she looked up she was surprised to see an old woman, quite unknown to her, drawing out thread[3] as she basked in the sun by the burnside. There was nothing remarkable about her except the length and thickness of her lips; but she was sitting on a self-bored[4] stone.

The girl rose with a friendly greeting, but could not help asking the old dame what had made her so "lang lippit".

"Spinning thread, ma hinnie," said the old woman, pleased with her friendliness and by no means resenting the question.

"Ah," said the girl, "I should be spinning too, but it's a' to no purpose. I'll ne'er dae ma task."

At once the old woman offered to do it for her and the girl ran off, overjoyed, to fetch her lint and hand it over; but when she asked her benefactor's name and when she would call for the yarn there was no reply. The old woman had vanished. Much bewildered, she wandered round for a time and finally fell asleep on the knoll.

When she awoke it was evening. Causleen, the evening star was shining and as she watched the moon rise the lassie was startled by the sound of a voice which seemed to come from a self-bored stone close-by. Laying her ear to it, she distinctly heard the words, "Little kens the wee lassie on the braeheid that my name's Habetrot."[5] Looking through the hole she saw her old friend walking up and down in a deep cavern among a group of spinsters all seated on colladie stones[6] and busy with distaff and spindle. An unsightly company they were, with lips disfigured like old Habetrot's. One of them who sat reeling the yarn had grey eyes that seemed to be starting from her head, and a long hooked nose. As she reeled she counted:

"Ae cribbie, twa cribbie, haith cribbie thou's ane; ae cribbie, twa cribbie, haith cribbie thou's twa."[7] So she continued until she had counted cut, hank and slip.

Habetrot addressed this singular being as Scantlie[8] Mab, telling her to bundle up the yarn for it was time the young lassie gave it to her mother. Very soon, to the girl's delight, Habetrot appeared and placed the yarn in her hands.

"Oh," cried she, "what can I do for ye in return?"

"Naething, naething," was the answer; "but dinna tell yer mither whae spun the yarn."

Scarcely believing her good fortune, the girl ran home to find her mother bedded for the night, but she had been making sausters and hanging them up in the lum to dry. Hungry after her long day the girl took them down and fried them, sauster after sauster, until they were finished. Then she too went to bed.

Next morning the mother was first up. Coming into the kitchen, she found her sausters all gone, but seven smooth hanks of yarn lay on the kitchen table. She ran out of the house crying:

> Ma dochter's spun se'en, se'en, se'en,
> Ma dochter's eaten se'en, se'en, se'en,
> And all before daylicht!

A laird who was riding by stopped to ask what might be the matter, on which she broke out again:

> Ma dochter's spun se'en, se'en, se'en,
> Ma dochter's eaten se'en, se'en, se'en,

"and if ye dinna believe me, come in and see."

The laird's curiosity was aroused, and when he had gone into the cottage and seen the yarn he asked to see the spinner also. When the blushing girl was dragged in he instantly fell in love with her, declaring that he wanted a wife and had long been looking for a bonny lass who was a good spinner.

So their troth was plighted and the wedding followed, the bride hiding her anxiety over the spinning tasks that would surely follow.[9] As soon as she got the chance, she was off again to the knoll beside the burn, and once again old Habetrot appeared.

"Bring your bonny bridegroom to my cell," she said. "When he sees what comes o' spinning he'll ne'er tie you to the wheel."

Next day the girl led her husband to the knoll and bade him look through the self-bored stone. Great was his surprise to see Habetrot dancing and jumping over her rock singing to her sisterhood, while they kept time with their spindles:

> We who live in dreary den
>   Are both rank and foul to see,
> Hidden frae the glorious sun
>   That leems all fair earth's canopie;
> Ever must our evenings lone
>   Be spent on the colludie-stone.
> Cheerless is the evening grey
>   When Causleen has died away,
> But ever bright and ever fair
>   Are they who breathe the evening air;
> And lean upon the self-bored stone
>   Unseen by all but me alone.

F

"Whae's keekin' at the stane?" asked Scantlie Mab.

"Ane whom I bid to come here at this hour," said Habetrot, and opening a door hidden in the root of a tree she welcomed the visitors.

The laird was amazed by the weird company. He went round asking each one the cause of their deformed mouths and each

answered, with a twist of the lips, that it was "a' occasioned by spinning". But instead of the word "occasioned" one grunted "nakasind", the next muttered "owkassand" and another whined "o-a-s'-in'd", and this caused him great alarm. So when Habetrot hinted that the same deformity would overtake his wife if he expected her to spin, he vowed that never again would she touch distaff or wheel.

So the young wife spent her days wandering in the meadows or riding behind her husband over the hills, while all the flax grown on their land was sent to be spun into thread by old Habetrot.

NOTES

1. Habetrot follows the second spinning-tale pattern in which the helper is benevolent and the name-guessing incidental. The formula runs: "Task assigned because of mother's boasting—magic spinning by deformed witches—sight of deformity leads to permanent release from spinning." Versions are found in Norway and Lithuania as well as in Grimm's *Household Tales*.

2. So many Scottish tales begin very early on a spring morning that the definitive description of this peaceful hour must be quoted. It occurs in *The Complaynt of Scotland*, (c.1548): "... the gayslings cryit Quhilk, Quhilk and the dukes cryit Quaik, and the huddie crauis cryit Varrock, Varrock, and the turtil began to greet quhen the cushet zoulet, the titlene followit the gowk and gart her sing Guk-guk, the doo croutit her sad sangs soundit like sorrow. The mavis made mirth for to mock the merle, the laverock made melody up hie in the skyis. The lint-white sang counterpoint when the owzel yelpit; the gowd-spink chantit, the rede-shank cryit My fut, my fut . . ."
   Summer, the writer concludes, "hed nother temperance nor tune".

3. Spinners constantly licked their fingers as they drew the thread out of the distaff.

4. A water-worn stone said to cover the entrance to the fairies' underground dwellings. Small stones of this kind were sometimes hung by cords to bed curtains as a cure for nightmares.

5. In the old days, when spinning was the constant employment of women, the spinning wheel had its presiding genius or fairy. Her Border name was Habetrot (W. Henderson, *Folk-lore*). She may have a long heredity. The Greek Athene carried spindle and distaff, and as the Roman Minerva she was patron and protector of all who practised the arts of spinning and weaving. Altars to her were set up all over Roman-occupied Scotland and remained to mystify the country people long after the Romans left. Old Habetrot, sunning herself by the burnside, may be the final, diminished glimpse of the august goddess.
   She makes another odd appearance in an ancient cure for certain diseases. The sufferer was counselled to wear a sark made out of lint grown in "a Field dunged by the Farm dung-heap that has not been renewed for forty years, and full of Bramlin ('a speckled worm found in old dunghills') spun by a person of the name of Habbytrot, wove by an honest weaver, bleached by an honest bleacher in an honest miller's mill dam, sewed by an honest taylor".

6. White quartz stones usually found in running water.
7. This was the guiding enumeration when reeling yarn on to a hand reel. "Ae cribbie" was once round the reel on a three-foot measure, the reel being about eighteen inches long. Twelve cuts made a slip.
8. Scantlie means niggardly, an appropriate nickname for Mab, whose function clearly was that of stock-taker.
9. She had good cause for anxiety—in the Highlands it was not out of the way for the laird's household to be equipped with twenty-four pairs of sheets, all spun at home. The Borders would not be far behind.

Peerifool

Place: Orkney.
Source: *County Folklore* (Orkney and Shetland).
    In this tale both the spinning types appear along with giant-killing and other motifs. It is an interesting, if not entirely successful, example of varied combinations.

There was once a king and queen in Rousay who had three daughters. The king died, and the queen was living in a small house with her daughters. They kept a cow and a kail yard;[1] they found their cabbage was all being taken away, and the eldest daughter said to the queen that she would take a blanket about her and would sit and watch what was going away with the kail. So when night came she went out to watch.

In a short time a very big giant came into the yard; he began to cut the kail and throw it into a big cubby. So he cut till he had it well filled.

The princess was always asking him why he was taking her mother's kail. He was saying to her, if she was not quiet he would take her too.

As soon as he had filled his cubby he took her by a leg and an arm and threw her on top of his cubby of kail and away he went with her.

When he got home he told her what work she had to do. She had to milk the cow and put her up to the hills called Bloodfield, and then she had to take wool, and wash and tease it and comb and card, and spin and make claith.

When the giant went out she milked the cow and put her to the hills. Then she put on the pot and made porridge to herself. As she was supping it, a great many peerie yellow-headed folk came running, calling out to give them some. She said:

> Little for one, and less for two,
> And never a grain have I for you.

When she came to work the wool, none of that work could she do at all.

The giant came home at night and found she had not done her work. He took her and began at her head, and peeled the skin off all the way down her back and over her feet. Then he threw her on the couples among the hens.[2]

The same adventure befell the second girl. If her sister could do little with the wool, she could do less.

When the giant came home he found her work not done. He began at the crown of her head and peeled a strip of skin all down her back and over her feet, and threw her on the couples beside her sister. They lay there and could not speak nor come down.

The next night the youngest princess said she would take a blanket about her and go to watch what had gone away with her sisters. Ere long, in came a giant with a big cubby, and began to cut the kail. She was asking why he was taking her mother's kail. He was saying if she would not be quiet he would take her too.

He took her by a leg and an arm and threw her on top of his cubby, and carried her away.

Next morning he gave her some work as he had given her sisters. When he was gone she milked the cow and put her to the high hills. Then she put on the pot and made porridge to herself. When the peerie yellow-headed folk came asking for some she told them to get something to sup with. Some got heather cows and some got broken dishes; some got one thing and some another and they all got some of her porridge.[3]

After they were all gone a peerie yellow-headed boy came in and asked her if she had any work to do; he could do any work with wool. She said she had plenty but would never be able to pay him for it. He said all he was asking for it was to tell him his name. She thought that would be easy to do, and gave him the wool.

When it was getting dark an old woman came in to ask her for lodging. The princess said she couldn't give her that, but asked her if she had any news. But the old woman had none, and went away to lie out.

There was a high knowe near the place and the old woman sat under it for shelter. She found it very warm. She was always climbing up and when she came to the top she heard someone inside saying, "Tease, teasers, tease; card, carders, card; spin, spinners, spin, for Peerifool, Peerifool is my name."

There was a crack in the knowe and light coming out. She looked in and saw a great many peerie folk working, and a peerie yellow-headed boy running round and calling out what she had heard. The old woman thought she would get lodging if she went to give this news, so she came back and told the princess the whole of it.

The princess went on saying "Peerifool, peerifool" till the yellow-headed boy came with all the wool made into claith. He asked what was his name, and she guessed names, and he jumped about and said No. At last she said, "Peerifool is your name," and he threw down the wool and ran away very angry.

As the giant was coming home he met a great many peerie yellow-headed folk, some with their eyes hanging out on their cheeks, and some with their tongues hanging on their breasts. He asked them what was the matter. They told him it was working so hard pulling wool so fine. He said he had a good wife at home, and if she was safe never would he allow her to do any work again.

When he came home she was safe, and had a great many webs lying all ready, and he was very kind to her.

Next day, when he was out she found her sisters, and took them down from the couples. She put the skin on their backs again, and she put her eldest sister in a cazy, and put all the fine things she could find with her, and grass on top.

When the giant came home she asked him to take the cazy to her mother with some food for the cow. He was so pleased with her he would do anything for her, and took it away. Next day she did the same with her other sister. She told him she would have the last of the food she had to send to her mother for the cow ready next night, but she herself was going a bit from home, and would leave it for him. She got into the cazy with all the fine things she could find, and covered herself with grass. He took the cazy and carried it to the queen's house. She and her daughters had a big boiler of boiling water ready. They couped it about him when he was under the window, and that was the end of the giant.

NOTES

1. In true folk tales kings and queens live as farmers. The queen is knowledgeable about livestock and the king often opens the door to travellers.
2. The hens would roost in the rafters.
3. A shepherd on Loch Ericht, troubled by fairies eating his porridge while it cooled, had the same idea. He made tiny wooden bowls and spoons to match, filled the bowls with porridge and set them beside his own. The fairies duly co-operated.

Rashiecoat

Place: Fife.
Source: Robert Chambers, *Popular Rhymes of Scotland*.

A Scottish variant of Cinderella. A folk-tale corresponding to this is to be found "diffused through every intervening country from the Himalayas to Ireland . . . . the lowlanders of North Britain also possess it", the oldest belonging to tenth century China. It is worth noting that Rashiecoat, as a good Presbyterian, does not escape to anything so frivolous as a ball.

Rashiecoat was a king's dochter, and her faither wanted her to be married; but she didna like the man. Her faither said she bud tak' him, and she didna ken what to do. Sae she gaed awa' to speer at the hen-wife.

The hen-wife says: "Say ye winna tak' him unless they gie you a coat o' the beaten gowd."

Weel, they ga'e her a coat o' the beaten gowd, but she didna want to tak' him for a' that; sae she gaed to the hen-wife again, and the hen-wife says: "Say ye winna tak' him unless they gie you a coat made o' the feathers o' a' the birds o' the air."

But the king sent a man wi' a great heap o' corn and the man cried to a' the birds o' the air: "Ilka bird tak' up a pea and put

down a feather. Ilka bird tak' up a pea and put down a feather."
Sae ilka bird took up a pea and put down a feather; and they
took a' the feathers and made a coat o' them and ga'e it to Rashiecoat; but she didna want to tak' him for a' that.

Weel, she gaed to the hen-wife again and speered what she
should do; and the hen-wife says: "Say ye winna tak' him unless
they gie you a coat o' rashes and a pair o' slippers."

Weel, they ga'e her a coat o' rashes and a pair o' slippers but
she didna want to tak' him for a' that. Sae she gaed to the hen-
wife again, and the hen-wife said she couldna help her ony
mair.

Weel, she left her faither's hoose and gaed far, and far, and
farer nor I can tell; and she cam' to a king's house and she gaed
in till't. And they speered at her what she was seeking, and she
said she was seeking service; and they ga'e her service and set
her into the kitchen to wash dishes and tak' out the ass and a'
that.

Whan the Sabbath day cam', they a' ga'ed to the kirk and left
her at hame to cook the dinner. And there was a fairy cam' to her
and telt her to put on her coat o' the beaten gowd and gang to
the kirk. And she said she couldna gang for she had to cook the
dinner; but the fairy telt her to gang and she would cook the
dinner for her.

And she said:

> Ae peat gar anither peat burn,
> Ae spit gar anither spit turn,
> Ae pat gar anither pat play,
> Let Rashiecoat gang to the kirk the day.

Sae Rashiecoat put on her coat o' the beaten gowd and gaed
awa' to the kirk. And the king's son fell in love wi' her; but she
cam' hame afore the kirk scaled and he couldna find oot wha she
was. And whan she cam' hame she fand the dinner cookit and
naebody kent she had been oot.

Weel, the neist Sabbath day the fairy cam' again and telt her
to put on the coat o' feathers o' a' the birds o' the air, an' gang to
the kirk, an' she would cook the dinner for her. Sae she put on the
coat o' feathers and gaed to the kirk and she cam' oot afore it
scaled and the king's son saw her gaun oot and he gaed oot too;

but he couldna fin' oot wha she was. An' she got hame and took off the coat o' feathers and fand the dinner cookit, and naebody kent she had been oot.

An' the neist Sabbath day the fairy cam' till her again and tell't her to put on the coat o' rashes an' the pair o' slippers and gang to the kirk again. Aweel, she did it a', an' this time the king's son sat near the door, and when he saw Rashiecoat slippin' oot afore the kirk scaled he slippit oot too, and grippit her. She got away frae him and ran hame but she lost ane o' her slippers an' he took it up. And he gar'd cry through a' the country that onybody that could get the slipper on, he would marry them.

Sae a' the leddies o' the court tried to get the slipper on, and it wadna fit nane o' them. And the auld hen-wife cam' an' fuss her dochter to try an' get it on, an' she nippit her fit an' clippit her fit an' got it on that way. Sae the king's son was going to marry her.

He was takin' her awa' to marry her, ridin' on a horse an' her ahint him; an' they cam' to a wood an' there was a bird sittin' on a tree. As they gaed by the bird said:

> Nippit fit an' clippit fit
> Ahint the king's son rides;
> But bonny fit an' pretty fit
> Ahint the cauldron hides.

When the king's son heard this he flang aff the hen-wife's dochter an' cam' hame again an' lookit ahint the cauldron, an' there he fand Rashiecoat greetin' for her slipper. He tried her fit wi' the slipper an' it gaed on fine.

Sae he married her,

> An' they lived happy and died happy
> An' never drank out o' a dry cappy.

The Milk-White Doo

Place: "Familiar in every Scottish nursery in the eighteenth century."

Source: Robert Chambers, *Popular Rhymes of Scotland*.

"There is no folk-story more widely spread than that of Grimm's Machandel-Baum (Juniper tree)... it is the Milk White Doo of Scotland, the Asterinos and Pulja of modern Greece. Goethe's Marguerite sings a snatch from it... the Bechuanas have a form of the myth." "Mythology and Fairy Tales", *Fortnightly Review*, May 1873.

There was once a man that wrought in the fields and had a wife, and a son, and a dochter. One day he caught a hare and took it hame to his wife and bade her make it ready for his dinner. While it was on the fire the gudewife aye tasted and tasted at it, till she had tasted a' away, and then she didna ken what to do for her gudeman's dinner. So she cried in Johnie, her son, to come and get his head kaimed; and when she was kaiming his head she slew him, and put him into the pat.

Well the gudeman cam hame to his dinner, and his wife set down Johnie well boiled to him; and when he was eating he takes up a fit, and says: "That's surely my Johnie's fit."

"Sic nonsense! it's ane o' the hare's," says the gudewife.

Syne he took up a hand, and says: "That's surely my Johnie's hand."

"Ye're havering, gudeman; it's anither o' the hare's feet."

So when the gudeman had eaten his dinner, little Katy, Johnie's sister, gathered a' the banes and put them in below a stane at the cheek o' the door:

> Where they grew, and they grew,
> To a milk-white doo,
> That took to its wings,
> And away it flew.

And it flew till it cam to where twa women were washing claes, and it sat down on a stane, and cried:

> Pew, pew
> My minny me slew,
> My daddy me chew,
> My sister gathered my banes,
> And put them between twa milk-white stanes;
> And I grew, and I grew,
> To a milk-white doo,
> And I took to my wings and away I flew.

"Say that owre again, my bonny bird, and we'll gie ye a' thir claes," says the women.

> Pew, pew,
> My minny me slew,
> My daddy me chew,

> My sister gathered my banes,
> And put them between twa milk-white stanes;
> And I grew, and I grew
> To a milk-white doo,
> And I took to my wings and away I flew.

And it got the claes; and then it flew till it cam to a man counting a great heap o' siller, and it sat down and cried:

> Pew, pew,
> My minny me slew,
> My daddy me chew,
> My sister gathered my banes,
> And put them between twa milk-white stanes;
> And I grew, and I grew
> To a milk-white doo,
> And I took to my wings, and away I flew.

"Say that again, my bonny bird, and I'll gie ye a' this siller," says the man.

> Pew, pew,
> My minny me slew,
> My daddy me chew,
> My sister gathered my banes,
> And put them between twa milk-white stanes;
> And I grew, and I grew,
> To a milk-white doo,
> And I took to my wings and away I flew.

And it got the siller; and syne it flew till it cam to twa millers grinding corn, and it cried:

> Pew, pew,
> My minny me slew,
> My daddy me chew,
> My sister gathered my banes,
> And put them between twa milk-white stanes;
> And I grew, and I grew,
> To a milk-white doo,
> And I took to my wings and away I flew.

Say that again, my bonny bird, and I'll gie ye this millstane," says the miller.

Pew, pew,
My minny me slew,
My daddy me chew,
My sister gathered my banes,
And put them between twa milk-white stanes;
And I grew, and I grew,
To a milk-white doo,
And I took to my wings and away I flew.

And it gat the mill-stane; and syne it flew till it lighted on its father's house-top. It threw sma' stanes down the lum, and Katy cam out to see what was the matter; and the doo threw a' the claes to her. Syne the father cam out, and the doo threw a' the siller to him. And syne the mother cam out, and the doo threw down the millstone upon her and killed her. And at last it flew away; and after that the gudeman and his dochter

Lived happy, and died happy,
And never drank out of a dry cappy.

NOTE

1. Told all over Europe. The pattern usually falls into four parts: "Murder of boy by stepmother—Burial by sister and first transformation into a bird—Revenge on stepmother and gifts for father and sister—Second transformation, after stepmother's death, back to human shape."

In the Scottish version the tale stops before the second transformation. Perhaps the happy ending was too rare in actual experience even to be brought into a story.

The Wal at the Warld's End

Place: Fife.
Source: Robert Chambers, *Popular Rhymes of Scotland.*

A Tale of the Wolf at the Warldis End (wolf being doubtless a misprint for well) is mentioned in *The Complaynt of Scotland,* c. 1548.

There was a king and a queen, and the king had a dochter and the queen had a dochter. The king's dochter was bonnie and guid-natured, and a'body liket her; and the queen's dochter was ugly and ill-natured, and naebody liket her. But the queen didna like the king's dochter and she wanted her awa'. Sae she sent her to the wal at the warld's end, to get a bottle o' water, thinking she would never come back. Weel, she took her bottle, and she gaed and gaed or she cam to a pownie that was tethered, and the pownie said to her:

> Flit me, flit me, my bonnie May,
> For I haena been flitted this seven year and a day.

And the king's dochter said: "Ay will I, my bonnie pownie, I'll flit ye."

Sae the pownie ga'e her a ride owre the Muir o' Heckle-pins.[1]

Weel, she gaed far and far and farer nor I can tell, or she cam to the wal at the warld's end; and when she cam to the wal, it was awfu' deep and she couldna get her bottle dippit. And as she was lookin' doon, thinkin' hoo to do, there lookit up to her three scaud men's heids,[2] and they said to her:

> Wash me, wash me, my bonnie May,
> And dry me wi' yer clean linen apron.

And she said, "Ay will I; I'll wash ye."

Sae she washed the three scaud men's heids, and dried them wi' her clean linen apron; and syne they took and dippit her bottle for her.

And the scaud men's heids said, the tane to the tither:

> Weird, brither, weird, what'll ye weird?

And the first ane said: "I weird that if she was bonnie afore, she'll be ten times bonnier."

And the second ane said: "I weird that ilka time she speaks, there'll a diamond and a ruby and a pearl drop oot o' her mouth."

And the third ane said: "I weird that ilka time she kaims[3] her heid, she'll get a peck o' gowd and a peck o' siller oot o' it."

Weel, she cam hame to the king's coort again, and if she was bonnie afore, she was ten times bonnier; and ilka time she opened her lips to speak there was a diamond and a ruby and a pearl drappit oot o' her mouth; and ilka time she kaimed her head, she gat a peck o' gowd and a peck o' siller oot o' it. And the queen was that vexed she didna ken what to do. Sae she sent her ain dochter to see if she could fa' in wi' the same luck.

Weel, the queen's dochter gaed and gaed or she cam to the pownie, an' the pownie said:

> Flit me, flit me, my bonnie May,
> For I haena been flitted this seven year and a day.

And the queen's dochter said: "Ou ye nasty beast, do ye think I'll flit ye? Do ye ken wha ye're speakin' till? I'm a queen's dochter."

Sae she wadna flit the pownie, and the pownie wadna gie her a ride ower the Muir o' Heckle-pins. And she had to gang on her bare feet, and the heckle-pins cuttit a' her feet, and she could hardly gang ava'.

Weel, she gaed far and far and farer nor I can tell, or she cam' to the wal at the warld's end. And the wal was deep, and she couldna get her bottle dippit; and as she was lookin' doon, thinkin' hoo to do, there lookit up at her three scaud men's heids, and they said till her:

> Wash me, wash me, my bonnie May,
> And dry me wi' yer clean linen apron.

And she said: "Ou ye nasty dirty beasts, div ye think I'm gaunie wash ye? Div ye ken wha ye're speakin' till? I'm a queen's dochter." Sae she wadna wash them, and they wadna dip her bottle for her.

And the scaud men's heids said the tane to the tither:

> Weird, brother, weird, what'll ye weird?

And the first ane said: "I weird that if she was ugly afore, she'll be ten times uglier."

And the second said: "I weird that ilka time she speaks there'll a puddock and a taid loup oot o' her mouth."

And the third ane said: "And I weird that ilka time she kaims her heid, she'll get a peck o' lice and a peck o' flechs oot o't."

Sae she gaed awa' hame again, and if she was ugly afore she was ten times uglier; and ilka time she opened her lips a puddock and a taid loupit oot o' her mouth; and ilka time she kaimed her head she got a peck o' lice and a peck o' flechs oot o' it. Sae they had to send her awa' frae the king's coort.

And there was a bonny young prince cam and married the

king's dochter; and the queen's dochter had to put up wi' an auld cobbler, and he lickit her ilka day wi' a leather strap.

NOTES

1. The Muir o' Heckle-pins. The same territory as Whinney-muir of the Lyke-wake Dirge where—"if hosen or shoon thou ne'er gavest nane, the whins shall prick thee to the bare bane". The hecklepin was the steel comb used by weavers to remove impurities from wool.
2. Sea urchins.
3. The comb is one of the oldest symbols in folklore, second only to the sword. Cut from a piece of bone with a flint knife, it may have been one of the first products of a new skill, and a marvel to the uninitiated, particularly if they saw sparks of gold fly from it when drawn through the hair on a frosty night. (See J. F. Campbell, *Popular Tales of the West Highlands*, Preface, p. lxxi.)

   Tolkien likens story to a bubbling cauldron in which "potent things" old, beautiful, terrible or comic are constantly being added, to simmer together through the ages and emerge at last in a new form. Those sparks of gold would probably go in about the end of the Stone Age, to be joined by Well-worshipping beliefs and emerge as a story flavoured by the cruel stepmother and magic journey themes.

The Black Bull o' Norroway[1]

Place: Lowlands, general.
Source: Robert Chambers, *Popular Rhymes of Scotland*.

In Norroway, langsyne, there lived a certain lady, and she had three dochters. The auldest o' them said to her mither: "Mither, bake me a bannock, and roast me a collop, for I'm gaun awa' tae spotch my fortune."

Her mither did sae; and the dochter gaed awa' to an auld witch washerwife and telled her purpose. The auld wife bade her stay that day, and gang and look out o' her back door, and see what she could see. She saw nocht the first day. The second day she did the same, and saw nocht. On the third day she looked again, and saw a coach and six coming alang the road. She ran in and telled the auld wife what she saw. "Aweel," quo' the auld wife, "yon's for you!" Sae they took her into the coach, and galloped aff.

The second dochter next says to her mither: "Mither, bake me a bannock and roast me a collop, for I'm gaun awa' tae spotch my fortune." Her mither did sae; and awa' she gaed to the auld wife, as her sister had dune. On the third day she looked out o' the back-door and saw a coach and four coming alang the road. "Aweel," quo' the auld wife. "Yon's for you." Sae they took her in and aff they set.

The third dochter says to her mither: "Mither, bake me a bannock, and roast me a collop, for I'm gaun awa' tae spotch my fortune." Her mither did sae; and awa' she gaed to the auld witch wife. She bade her look out o' her back door, and see what she could see. She did sae; and when she came back, said she saw nocht. The second day she did the same, and saw nocht. The third day she looked again, and said she saw nocht but a muckle Black Bull coming crooning alang the road. "Aweel," quo the auld wife, "yon's for you."

On hearing this she was next to distracted wi' grief and terror; but she was lifted up and set on his back, and awa' they went.

Aye they travelled, and on they travelled, till the lady grew faint wi' hunger.

"Eat out o' my right lug," says the Black Bull, "and drink out o' my left lug, and set by your leavings."

Sae she did as he said, and was wonderfully refreshed. And lang they gaed, and sair they rade, till they came in sight o' a very big and bonny castle. "Yonder we maun be this night," says the Bull, "for my auld brither lives yonder"; and presently they were at the place. They lifted her aff his back, and took her in, and sent him away to a park for the night.

In the morning, when they brought the Bull hame, they took the lady into a fine shining parlour, and gave her a beautiful apple,[2] telling her no to break it till she was in the greatest strait ever mortal was in, and that wad bring her out o't.

Again she was lifted on the Bull's back, and after she had ridden far, and farer than I can tell, they came in sight o' a far bonnier castle, and far farther awa' than the last. Says the Bull till her: "Yonder we maun be the night, for my second brither lives yonder"; and they were at the place directly. They lifted her down and took her in, and sent the Bull to the field for the night.

G

In the morning they took the lady into a fine and rich room, and gave her the finest pear she had ever seen, bidding her no' to

break it till she was in the greatest strait ever mortal could be in, and that wad get her out o't.

Again she was lifted and set on his back, and awa' they went. And lang they rade, and sair they rade, till they came in sight o' the far biggest castle, and far farthest they had yet seen. "We maun be yonder the night," says the Bull, "for my young brither lives yonder"; and they were there directly. They lifted her down, took her in, and sent the Bull to the field for the night.

In the morning they took her into a room, the finest of a', and gied her a plum, telling her no' to break it till she was in the greatest strait mortal could be in, and that wad get her out o't. Presently they brought home the Bull, set the lady on his back, and awa' they went.

And aye they rade, and on they rade, till they came to a dark and ugsome glen, where they stopped and the lady lighted down. Says the Bull to her: "Here ye maun stay till I gang and fight the deil. Ye maun seat yoursel' on that stane and move neither hand nor fit till I come back, else I'll never find ye again. And if everything round about ye turns blue, I hae beaten the deil; but should a' things turn red, he'll hae conquered me."

She sat hersel' down on the stane, and by-and-by a' round her turned blue. O'ercome wi' joy, she lifted the ae fit and crossed it owre the ither, sae glad was she that her companion was victorious. The Bull returned and sought for her, but could never find her.

Lang she sat, and aye she grat, till she wearied. At last she rase and gaed awa', she kendna whaur till. On she wandered till she came to a great hill o' glass that she tried a' she could to climb, but wasna able. Round the bottom o' the hill she gaed, sabbin' and seeking a passage owre, till at last she came to a smith's house; and the smith promised if she would serve him seven years he wad make her airn shoon, wherewi' she could climb owre the glassy hill.

At seven years' end she got her airn shoon, clamb the glassy hill, and chanced to come to the auld washerwife's habitation. There she was telled of a gallant young knight that had given in some bluidy sarks to wash, and whaever washed they sarks was to be his wife. The auld wife had washed till she was tired, and then she set to her dochter, and baith washed, and they washed and they better washed, in hopes of getting the young knight; but a' they could do, they couldna bring oot a stain. At length they set the stranger damosel to wark; and whenever she began, the stains came out pure and clean, and the auld wife made the knight believe it was her dochter had washed the sarks.

So the knight and the washer-wife's dochter were to be married, and the stranger damosel was distracted at the thought of it, for she was deeply in love wi' him. So she bethought her of her apple. Breaking it, she found it filled with gold and precious jewellery, the richest she had ever seen.

"All these," she said to the dochter, "I will give you on condition that you put off your marriage for ae day, and allow me to go into his room alone at night."

So she consented, but meanwhile the auld wife had prepared a sleeping draught, and given it to the knight wha drank it and never wakened till next morning.

The lee-lang night the damosel sabbed and sang:

> Seven lang years I served for thee,
> The glassy hill I clamb for thee,
> The bluidy shirt I wrang for thee;
> Wilt thou no wauken and turn to me?

Next day she kentna what do to for grief. She then brak the pear, and fan't filled wi' jewellery far richer than the contents o' the apple. Wi' thae jewels she bargained for permission to be a second night in the young knight's chamber; but the auld wife gied him anither sleeping drink, and again he sleepit till morning.

A' night she kept sighing and singing as before:

> Seven lang years I served for thee,
> The glassy hill I clamb for thee,
> The bluidy shirt I wrang for thee;
> Wilt thou no wauken and turn to me?

Still he sleepit, and she nearly lost hope a'thegethir. But that day when he was out at the hunting, somebody asked him what noise and moaning they had heard a' last night in his bedchamber. He said he heardna ony noise, but he resolved to keep waking that night to try what he could hear.

That being the third night, and the damosel being between hope and despair, she brak her plum, and it held far the richest jewellery of the three. She bargained as before; and the auld wife took in the sleeping drink to the young knight; but he telled her he couldna drink it again without sweetening. When she gaed awa' for some honey he poured it out and made the auld wife think he had drunk it.

They a' went to bed, and again the damosel began singing:

> Seven lang years I served for thee,
> The glassy hill I clamb for thee,
> The bluidy shirt I wrang for thee;
> Wilt thou no wauken and turn to me?

He heard, and turned to her.[3]

She telled him a' that had befa'en her, and he telled her a' that had happened to him. He caused the auld washerwife and her dochter to be punished; and they were married, and he and she are living happy till this day, for aught I ken.

NOTES

1. This tale is a variant on the Enchanted Husband theme, universal in folklore. The usual pattern runs: Girl betrothed to a monster, really a prince bespelled—Magic gifts—Girl disenchants but loses husband—Search encountering great obstacles—Recognition difficulty—Final reunion.

   This version more or less follows the pattern but the fact that the Prince disenchants himself, by means of a battle with the evil principle, is interesting in view of the Scottish preoccupation with the idea of man working out his own salvation.

   In the Tales, transformation to animal form did not mean loss of personality. From the moment he appears "crooning" down the road this Bull is a noble and a gentle creature, his dignity unimpaired even when he is put out to grass for the night at his brothers' castles.

2. In another version of this tale the Princess is given three nuts to crack in time of need. One contains a wee wifie carding, the next a wee wifie spinning and the third a wee wifie reeling.

3. "He heard and turned to her." Tolkien quotes those six words as an outstanding example of what he calls "the good catastrophe"—the sudden turn from disaster to joy that lifts the heart of the listener and marks a good fairy tale. J. R. R. Tolkien, *Tree and Leaf.*

The Paddo

Place: Dumfriesshire.
Source: Robert Chambers, *Popular Rhymes of Scotland.*
Narrator: Nurse Jenny of Hoddam.
Collector: Charles Kirkpatrick Sharpe.

This is another story on the enchanted bridegroom theme. The Frog Prince has references in ancient German literature and Scott claimed that it was told among the Tartars.

Andrew Lang points out that as a tribal totem the frog had a very ancient signification. (*Fortnightly Review*, May 1873.)

A poor widow was one day baking bannocks, and sent her dochter wi' a dish to the well to bring water. The dochter gaed and better gaed, till she came to the well, but it was dry. Now, what to do she didna ken, for she couldna gang back to her mother without water; sae she sat down by the side o' the well, and fell a-greeting.

A Paddo then came loup-loup-louping out o' the well and asked the lassie what she was greeting for; and she said she was greeting because there was nae water in the well.

"But," says the Paddo, "an ye'll be my wife I'll gie ye plenty o' water." And the lassie, no thinking that the poor beast could mean anything serious, said she would be his wife, for the sake o' getting the water.

So she got the water into her dish and gaed awa' hame to her mother and thought nae mair about the Paddo till that night, when, just as she and her mother were about to go to their beds, something came to the door, and when they listened they heard this sang:

> O open the door, my hinnie, my heart,
> O open the door, my ain true love;
> Remember the promise that you and I made,
> Down i' the meadow, where we twa met.

Says the mother to the dochter, "What noise is that at the door?"

"Hout," says the dochter, "it's naething but a filthy Paddo."

"Open the door," says the mother, "to the poor Paddo."

So the lassie opened the door, and the Paddo came loup-loup-louping in, and sat down by the ingle-side. Then he sings:

> O gie me my supper, my hinnie, my heart,
> O gie me my supper, my ain true love;
> Remember the promise that you and I made,
> Down i' the meadow, where we twa met.

"Hout," quo the dochter, "wad I gie a filthy Paddo his supper?"

"O ay," said the mother, "e'en gie the poor Paddo his supper."

So the Paddo got his supper; and after that he sings again:

O put me to bed, my hinnie, my heart,
O put me to bed, my ain true love;
Remember the promise that you and I made,
Down i' the meadow, where we twa met.

"Hout," quo the dochter, "wad I put a filthy Paddo to bed?"
"O ay," says the mother, "put the poor Paddo to his bed."
Then the Paddo sings again:

> Now fetch me an axe, my hinnie, my heart,
> Now fetch me an axe, my ain true love;
> Remember the promise that you and I made,
> Down i' the meadow, where we twa met.

The lassie wasna lang o' fetching the axe; and then the Paddo sang:

> Now chap aff my head, my hinnie, my heart,
> Now chap aff my head, my ain true love;
> Remember the promise that you and I made,
> Down i' the meadow, where we twa met.

Weel, the lassie chappit aff his head; and no sooner was that done than he started up the bonniest young prince that ever was seen. And the twa lived happy a' the rest o' their days.

The Red Etin

Place: Fife.
Source: Robert Chambers, *Popular Rhymes of Scotland*.
Collector: Peter Buchan.

This very old tale is mentioned in *The Complaynt of Scotland* (c. 1548). Sir David Lyndsay writes of amusing the young King James V with "money plesand story of the Red Etin".

The word Etin is derived from the Scandinavian *äetan* meaning giant.

This is the Scottish version of Jack the Giant Killer.

There were ance twa widows that lived ilk ane on a small bit o' ground, which they rented from a farmer. Ane of them had twa sons, and the other had ane; and by and by it was time for the wife that had twa sons to send them away to spouss their fortune.

So she told her eldest son ae day to take a can and bring her water from the well, that she might bake a cake for him; and however much or however little water he might bring, the cake would be big or sma' accordingly; and that cake was to be a' she could gie him when he went on his travels.

The lad gaed away wi' the can to the well and filled it wi' water; but the can being broken, the maist part o' the water had run out before he got back. So his cake was very sma'; yet sma' as it was, his mother asked if he was willing to take the half of it with her blessing, for if he chose to have the hale he would only get it wi' her curse. Thinking he might hae far to travel he said he would like the hale cake, come of his mother's malison what like; so she gave him the hale cake and her malison alang wi't.

Then he took his brither aside and gave him a knife to keep till he should come back, desiring him to look at it every morning. As lang as it continued to be clear he might be sure that the owner of it was well; but if it grew dim and rusty, then for certain some ill had befallen him.

So the young man set out to spouss his fortune. He gaed a' that day, and a' the next day; and on the third day, in the afternoon, he came to where a shepherd was sitting with a flock o' sheep. He gaed up to the shepherd and asked him wha the sheep belanged to; and the man answered:

> The Red Etin of Ireland
>   Ance lived in Bellygan,
> He stole King Malcolm's daughter,
>   The king of fair Scotland.
> He beats her, he binds her,
>   He lays her on a band;   .
> And every day he dings her
>   With a bright silver wand.
> Like Julian the Roman
> He's one that fears no man.
>
> It's said there's ane predestinate
>   To be his mortal foe;
> But that man is still unborn,
>   And lang may it be so.

The lad went on; and he had not gone far when he espied an old man with white locks herding a flock of swine. He gaed up to him and asked whose swine they were, and the man answered:

> The Red Etin of Ireland
>   Ance lived in Bellygan,

He stole King Malcolm's daughter,
   The king of fair Scotland.
He beats her, he binds her,
   He lays her on a band;
And ilka day he dings her
   With a bright silver wand.
Like Julian the Roman
He's one that fears no man.

It's said there's ane predestinate
   To be his mortal foe;
But that man is yet unborn,
   And lang may it be so.

The young man gaed on a bit farther and came to another very old man herding goats; and when he asked whose goats they were, the answer was:

The Red Etin of Ireland
   Ance lived in Bellygan,
He stole King Malcolm's daughter,
   The king of fair Scotland.
He beats her, he binds her,
   He lays her on a band;
And every day he dings her
   With a bright silver wand.
Like Julian the Roman
He's one that fears no man.

It's said there's ane predestinate
   To be his mortal foe;
But that man is yet unborn,
   And lang may it be so.

This old man told him to beware o' the next beasts that he should meet, for they were of a very different kind from any he had yet seen.

So he went on, and by and by he saw a multitude of very dreadful beasts, ilk ane o' them wi' twa heads, and on every head four horns. And he was sore frightened, and ran away from them as fast as he could; and glad was he when he came to a castle that stood on a hillock, wi' the door standing wide to the wa'.

He gaed into the castle for shelter, and there he saw an auld wife sitting by the kitchen fire. He asked if he could stay the

night; and the wife said he might, but it was not a good place
for him to be in as it belonged to the Red Etin, who was a very
terrible beast wi' three heads, that spared no living man he could
get hold of. The young man was sore afraid o' the beasts on the
outside of the castle, so he beseeched the old woman to conceal
him, and not tell the Etin that he was there. But he had not been
long in his hidy-hole before the awful Etin came in; and nae
sooner was he in, than he was heard crying:

> Snouk but and snouk ben,
> I find the smell of an earthly man;
> Be he living, or be he dead,
> His heart this night shall kitchen my bread.

The monster soon found the young man and pulled him from
his hole. But he told him that if he could answer him three
questions his life should be spared. The first was, Whether Ireland or Scotland was first inhabited? The second was, Whether
man was made for woman, or woman for man? The third was,
Whether men or brutes were made first? The lad not being able
to answer one of these questions, the Red Etin took a mell and
knocked him on the head, and turned him into a pillar of stone.

On the morning after this happened, the younger brither took
out the knife to look at it, and saw that it was a' brown wi' rust.
He told his mother that he also must go off on his travels, and
she asked him to take the can to the well for water, that she might
bake a cake for him. The can being broken, he brought hame as
little water as the other had done, and the cake was as little. But,
like his brither, he thought it best to have the hale cake, come o'
the malison what might.

So he gaed awa' and he came to the shepherd that sat wi' his
flock o' sheep, and asked him whose sheep they were. And the
shepherd said:

> The Red Etin of Ireland
> Ance lived in Bellygan,
> He stole King Malcolm's daughter,
> The king o' fair Scotland.
> He beats her, he binds her,
> He lays her on a band;
> And every day he dings her
> With a bright silver wand.

> Like Julian the Roman
> He's one that fears no man.
>
> It's said there's ane predestinate
>   To be his mortal foe;
> But that man is yet unborn,
>   And lang may it be so.

On he gaed till he met the auld man wi' his flock o' swine and asked whose swine they were; and he got the same answer:

> The Red Etin of Ireland
>   Ance lived in Bellygan,
> He stole King Malcolm's daughter,
>   The king of fair Scotland.
> He beats her, he binds her,
>   He lays her on a band;
> And every day he dings her
>   With a bright silver wand.
> Like Julian the Roman
> He's one that fears no man.
>
> It's said there's ane predestinate
>   To be his mortal foe;
> But that man is yet unborn,
>   And lang may it be so.

Syne the young man came to the auld goat herd. He gaed up as his brither had done and asked whose goats they were. And the goat-herd said:

> The Red Etin of Ireland
>   Ance lived in Bellygan,
> He stole King Malcolm's daughter
>   The king of fair Scotland.
> He beats her, he binds her,
>   He lays her on a band;
> And every day he dings her
>   With a bright silver wand.
> Like Julian the Roman
> He's one that fears no man.
>
> It's said there's ane predestinate
>   To be his mortal foe;
> But that man is yet unborn,
>   And lang may it be so.

By and by he came to where the dreadful beasts were, and running away from them he saw the castle on the hillock wi' its door wide to the wa'. The auld wife was still sitting by the kitchen fire and in spite of her warnings he begged her to give him a night's shelter and hide him from the Red Etin. But he had not been lang in his hidey-hole when the Etin was heard crying:

> Snouk but and snouk ben,
> I find the smell of an earthly man;
> Be he living, or be he dead,
> His heart this night shall kitchen my bread.

When he was found and dragged from his hole the lad was no more able to answer the questions than his brither had been; so he too was turned into a pillar of stone.

The other widow and her son heard of a' that had happened frae a fairy, and the third lad made up his mind to go on his travels and see if he could do onything to relieve his twa friends. His mother gave him a can to bring water frae the well that she might bake him a cake. And as he came back a raven owre abune his head cried to him to look and he would see the water running out. He was a lad o' sense, and he patched up the holes with clay, so he brought home enough water to bake a large cake. When his mother put it to him to take half the cake wi' her blessing, he took it rather than hae the hale wi' her malison; and yet the half was bigger than what the other lads had got a'the-gither.

So he gaed awa' on his journey; and after he had travelled a far way, he met an auld woman, that asked him if he would give her a bit of his bannock. And he said he would gladly do that; so he gave her a piece and she gied him a magical wand that she said might yet be of service if he took care to use it rightly. Then she told him a great deal that would happen to him, and what he ought to do in a' circumstances; and after that she vanished out o' his sight.

He gaed on a great way farther, and came to the old man herding his sheep; and when he asked whose sheep these were, the answer was:

> The Red Etin of Ireland
> Ance lived in Bellygan,
> He stole King Malcolm's daughter,
> The King of fair Scotland.

He beats her, he binds her,
　　He lays her on a band;
And every day he dings her
　　With a bright silver wand.
Like Julian the Roman
He's one that fears no man.

But now I fear his end is near,
　　And destiny at hand;
And you're to be, I plainly see,
　　The heir of all his land.

A great way farther on he found the auld man with the flock
of swine and asked whose swine they were. The swine herd said:

The Red Etin of Ireland
　　Ance lived in Bellygan,
He stole King Malcolm's daughter,
　　The king of fair Scotland.
He beats her, he binds her,
　　He lays her on a band;
And every day he dings her
　　With a bright silver wand.
Like Julian the Roman
He's one that fears no man.

But now I fear his end is near,
　　And destiny at hand;
And you're to be, I plainly see,
　　The heir of all his land.

On gaed the lad till he came to the auld goat-herd. He asked
whose the goats might be, and the answer was the same:

The Red Etin of Ireland
　　Ance lived in Bellygan;
He stole King Malcolm's daughter,
　　The king of fair Scotland.
He beats her, he binds her,
　　He lays her on a band,
And ilka day he dings her
　　With a bright silver wand.
Like Julian and Roman
He's one that fears no man.

But now I fear his end is near,
And destiny at hand;
And you're to be, I plainly see,
The heir of all his land.

When he came to the place where the monstrous beasts were standing, he did not stop nor run away, but went boldly through amongst them. One came up roaring with open mouth to devour him, but he struck it with his wand and laid it in an instant dead at his feet.

He soon came to the Etin's castle, where he knocked and was admitted. The auld woman that sat by the fire warned him of the terrible Etin, and what had been the fate of his twa friends; but he was not to be daunted.

Soon the monster came in saying:

> Snouk but and snouk ben,
> I find the smell of an earthly man;
> Be he living, or be he dead,
> His heart shall be kitchen to my bread.

He quickly spied the young man and bade him come forth on the floor. And then he put the three questions to him; but the young man had been told everything by the old woman, so he was able to answer them all; and the Etin knew that his power was gone.

Then the lad took an axe and cut off the monster's three heads, next he asked the old woman to show him where the king's daughter lay and she took him up stairs and opened many doors, and out of every door came a beautiful lady imprisoned by the Etin; and ane o' them was the king's daughter.

The old woman took him down, then, into a low room and there stood the stone pillars; but he had only to touch them wi' his wand and his two friends and neighbours started into life. And the hale o' the prisoners were overjoyed at their deliverance, which they all acknowledged as due to the prudent young man.

Next day they a' set out for the king's court, and a gallant company they made. And the king married his daughter to the lad that had delivered her, and gave a noble's daughter to ilk ane o' the other lads; and so they a' lived happy a' the rest o' their days.

V

JUST ANCE MAIR

"Tell us yon story again!"
"Hout, bairns, ye've heard it a hunnert times afore."
"Aye, but it's sic a fine ane—just ance mair!"
"Weel, weel; if ye'll a' promise to be guid. . . ."

A ND once started the flow of stories, rhymes, riddlums and quirk-
lums[1] would probably hold out till bedtime, for "a copious supply
of song, tale and drollery" was basic equipment for any nurse or
grandmother worthy of the name. Here at least the children of past
centuries were fortunate.

Not that all was happy drollery. What with bogles, monsters, the
Hag Macniven, the Gyre Carlin and Auld Nick, the winter shadows
must have seemed alive with perils. Scottish children were reared on
strong meat, but they could take it. Even that Strange Visitor, feared
by their elders as the Last Enemy, was hailed in the nursery with more
delight than terror as he materialised, bit by gruesome bit, to claim a
victim for the kirkyard mool.

And the real fun was never far away. It breaks out in a group of
bairn-tales varying from crude nonsense to such enchantments as the
wee bunnock, the wifie and her kidie, and the marriage of Robin
Redbreast as recounted to his small brothers and sisters by Robert
Burns. These tales flickered through daily life like sunlight, always
ready to divert or console; but their accepted time was the winter
forenicht.[2] Those hours between the failing of light and the day's end
gathered all children to the fireside and gave the labourer, honest
"Jok-upon-land", almost his only chance to foregather with his
family. So the cry, "just ance mair" would be heard in the high
narrow-windowed, lamp-lit nurseries of lairds' houses, such as that in
which Mammy Jenny's recitals drew applause and admiring hugs from
her demanding audience; or it would add to the general clamour of
the "peasant's hovel", packed with humanity and hazy with peat
reek.[3]

But whatever the background, the magic of the tales was the
same.

H

NOTES

1. A quirklum was a little mathematical puzzle, as opposed to a riddlum or conundrum.

2. The forenicht, being the time between dusk and going to bed, only existed in winter. In the long summer light work in the fields went on till bed time.

   Other wonderfully descriptive terms were used for times of the day and year.

   Midnight was "the how o' the nicht" or even better, in suggesting silence as well as darkness, "the how-dumb-deid o' the nicht"; "the how o' the year" meant the depth of winter. There was also "the dark o' the moon", significant in both human and animal life.

   The hours between dawn and sunrise were known as the "neb o' the morning", the time when the hoar frost breaks in winter and the coldest part of the night. To "bide in bed till the neb's aff the morning" was to pamper oneself.

   On certain ancient charters spring and autumn were called "the season of grass" and "the season of corn".

3. "Rows of turf and heather were placed along the cross-spars of the roof, while the fire of peats blazed exactly in the middle of the floor and sent its smoke through an aperture in the roof. In certain states of weather the smoke formed a thick cloud above the head so that the joints and rafters were as black and glossy as a looking glass . . ." Here "in the winter forenichts the old men kept the noisy gytlings quiet with tales, and their wives sang and laughed and span the rock amid the clouds of peat-reek. The comfort, in the shivering days of winter, was much greater than we suppose." The Rev. Robert Simpson, *The Cottars of the Glen.*

The Wifie and her Kidie

Place: Aberdeenshire.
Source: *Folklore Journal*, vol. 2, 1884.
Narrator: Mrs. Moir of Old Meldrum.
Collector: The Rev. Walter Gregor.

There wiz a wifie, an she sweipit her hoosie clean an fair, an she fan twal pennies. An she gaed till the market, an she bocht a kid. An she said: "Kid, kid, rin hame, leuk the hoose an come again till I gedder a puckle sticks to my fair firie."

"Niver a lenth," said the kid, "will I rin hame, leuk the hoose, an come again; ye can dee't yersel'."

An the wifie said to the dog: "Dog, dog, bite kid; kid winna rin hame, leuk the hoose an come again, till I gedder a puckle sticks to my fair firie."

"Niver a lenth," said the dog, "will I bite the kid; the kid niver did me ony ill."

"Stick, stick, ding dog: dog winna bite kid, kid winna rin hame, leuk the hoose an come again, till I gedder a puckle sticks for my fair firie."

"Niver a lenth," said the stick, "will I ding dog; dog niver did me ony ill."

"Fire, fire, burn stick; stick winna ding dog, dog winna bite kid, kid winna rin hame, leuk the hoose an come again, till I gedder a puckle sticks to my fair firie."

"Niver a lenth," said the fire; "stick niver did me ony ill."

"Watter, watter, quench fire; fire winna burn stick, stick winna ding dog, dog winna bite kid, kid winna rin hame, leuk the hoose an come again, till I gedder a puckle sticks to my fair firie."

"Niver a lenth," said the watter, "will I quench fire. Fire niver did me ony ill."

"Ox, ox, drink watter; watter winna quench fire, fire winna burn stick, stick winna beat dog, dog winna bite kid, kid winna rin hame, leuk the hoose an come again, till I gedder a puckle sticks to my fair firie."

"Niver a lenth," said the ox; "watter niver did me ony ill."

"Aix, aix, kill ox; ox winna drink watter, watter winna quench fire, fire winna burn stick, stick winna ding dog, dog winna bite kid, kid winna rin hame, leuk the hoose an come again, till I gedder a puckle sticks to my fair firie."

"Niver a lenth," said the aix; "ox never did me ony ill."

"Smith, smith, smee aix; aix winna kill ox, ox winna drink watter, watter winna quench fire, fire winna burn stick, stick winna ding dog, dog winna bite kid, kid winna rin hame, leuk the hoose an come again, till I gedder a puckle sticks to my fair firie."

"Niver a lenth," says the smith; "aix niver did me ony hairm."

"Rope, rope, hang smith; smith winna smee aix, aix winna kill ox, ox winna drink watter, watter winna quench fire, fire winna burn stick, stick winna ding dog, dog winna bite kid, kid winna rin hame, leuk the hoose an come again, till I gedder a puckle sticks to my fair firie."

"Niver a lenth," says the rope, "will I hang smith; smith niver did me ony ill."

"Moosie, moosie, gnaw rope; rope winna hang smith, smith winna smee aix, aix winna kill ox, ox winna drink watter, watter winna quench fire, fire winna burn stick, stick winna ding dog, dog winna bite kid, kid winna rin hame, leuk the hoose an come again, till I gedder a puckle sticks to my fair firie."

"Niver a lenth," says the moosie, "will I gnaw rope; rope niver did me ony ill."

Noo, a' this time the cattie wiz sittin' i' the ingle-neuk singin' a sang till hersel'.[1]

So the wifie said: "Bonnie cattie, gin ye wud tak moosie I wud gie ye some fine milk an breed t'yersel'."

So the cattie t' the moosie, an the moosie t' the rope, an the rope t' the smith, an the smith t' the aix, and the aix t' the ox, an the ox t' the watter, and the watter t' the fire, an the fire t' the stick, an the stick t' the dog, and the dog t' the kid, an the kid ran hame, leukit the hoose an cam again till the wifie gedderit a puckle sticks till her fair firie.

NOTE

1. According to tradition, the cat's song would be:

Thr-r-um, thr-r-um,
Thr-r-ee thr-r-reds and a thr-r-rum.

There have been some notable cats in Scottish annals, including Crumwhull's Gib, and Barr's cat which became a proverb for anything bigger than it ought to be.

The Wee Bunnock

Place: Ayrshire.
Source: Robert Chambers, *Popular Rhymes of Scotland.*
Narrator: "A venerable person" born in 1704. She had "a great store of legends which she related as she sat spinning by her fireside with youngsters clustered round her". One of these, her grandson, repeated the tale to Robert Chambers, "the speech of the aged narrator faithfully preserved".

There lived an auld man and an auld wife at the side o' a burn. They had twa kye, five hens and a cock, a cat and twa' kittlins. The auld man lookit after the kye, and the auld wife span on the tow-rock. The kittlins aft grippit at the auld wife's spindle as it tussled owre the hearth-stane. "Sho, sho," she wad say, "gae wa'."

Ae day after parritch time she thought she wad hae a bunnock. Sae she bakit twa aitmeal bunnocks, and set them to the fire to harden. After a while, the auld man came in and sat down aside the fire, and takes ane o' the bunnocks, and snappit it through the middle. When the tither ane sees this, it rins aff as fast as it could, and the auld wife after it wi' the spindle in the tae hand and the tow-rock in the tither. But the wee bunnock wan awa' and oot o' sight, and ran till it came to a guid muckle thack house, and ben it ran boldly to the fireside; and there were three tailors sitting on a muckle table.[1] When they saw the wee bunnock come ben, they jumpit up, and gat in ahint the goodwife that was cardin' tow ayont the fire.

"Hout," quo' she, "be na fleyt; it's but a wee bunnock. Grip it, and I'll gie ye a sup milk till't."

Up she gets wi' the tow-cards and the tailor wi' the goose, and the twa prentices, the ane wi' the muckle shears, and the tither wi' the lawbrod; but it jinkit them, and ran round about the

fire;[2] and ane o' the prentices, thinking to snap it wi' the shears, fell i' the ase-pit. The tailor cuist the goose, and the good-wife the tow-cards; but a' wadna do.

The bunnock wan awa', and ran till it came to a wee house at the roadside; and in it rins, and there was a weaver sittin' on the loom, and the wife winnin' a clue o' yarn.

"Tibby," quo' he, "what's tat?"

"Oh," quo' she, "it's a wee bunnock."

"It's weel come," quo' he, "for our sowens were but thin the day. Grip it, my woman; grip it,"

"Aye," quo' she, "what recks! That's a clever bunnock. Kep, Willie; kep, man!"

"Hout," quo' Willie, "cast the clue at it."

But the bunnock whippit round about and but the floor, and aff it gaed and ower the knowe like a new-tarred sheep or a daft yell cow. And forrit it rins to the niest house and ben to the fireside; and there was the goodwife kirnin'.

"Come awa', wee bunnock," quo' she; "I'se hae ream and bread the day."

But the wee bunnock whippit round about the kirn and the wife after't and i' the hurry she had near-hand coupit the kirn. And afore she got it set right again the wee bunnock was aff and down the brae to the mill; and in it ran.

The miller was siftin' meal i' the trough; but, lookin' up, "Ay," quo' he, "it's a sign o' plenty when ye're rinnin' aboot and naebody to look after ye! But I like a bunnock and cheese. Come your wa's ben and I'll gie ye a night's quarters."

But the bunnock wadna trust itsel' wi' the miller and his cheese. Sae it turned and ran its wa's out; but the miller didna fash his head wi't.[3]

So it toddled awa' and ran till it cam' to the smithy; and in it rins and up to the studdy.

The smith was making horse-nails. Quo' he, "I like a bicker o' guid yill and a weel-toastit bunnock. Come your wa's in by here."

But the bunnock was frightened when it heard about the yill, and turned and aff as hard as it could, and the smith after it and cuist the hammer.

But it whirlt awa' and oot o' sight in a crack, and ran till it came to a farm-house wi' a guid muckle peat-stack at the end o't. Ben it rins to the fireside.

The goodman was clovin' lint and the goodwife was hecklin'. "O Janet," quo' he, "there's a wee bunnock; I'se hae the hauf o't."

"Weel, John, I'se hae the tither hauf. Hit it ower the back wi' the clove." But the bunnock played jink-aboot.

"Hout-tout," quo' the wife, and gart the heckle flee at it. But it was owre clever for her.

Aff and up the burn it ran to the niest house and whirlt its wa's ben to the fireside. The goodwife was stirrin' the sowens and the goodman plettin' sprit-binnings for the kye.

"Ho, Jock," quo' the goodwife, "come here. Thou's aye crying about a wee bunnock. Here's ane. Come in, haste ye, and I'll help ye to grip it."

"Aye, mither, whaur is't?"

"See there. Rin ower that side."

But the bunnock ran in ahint the goodman's chair. Jock fell among the sprits. The goodman cuist a binning and the goodwife the spurtle, but it was ower clever for Jock and her baith. It was aff and out o' sight in a crack, and through among the whins and down the road to the neist house and ben to the fireside.

The folk were just sittin' doon to their sowens and the goodwife scartin' the pat.

"Losh," quo' she, "there's a wee bunnock come in to warm itsel' at our fireside."

"Steek the door," quo' the gudeman, "and we'll try to get a grup o't."

When the bunnock heard that it ran but the house, and they after't wi' their spunes, and the goodman cuist his bunnat. But it whirlt awa', and ran, and better ran till it came to another house.

When it gaed ben the folk were just gaun to their beds. The goodman was castin' aff his breeks, and the goodwife rakin' the fire.

"What's tat?" quo' he.

"O," quo she, "it's a wee bunnock."

Quo' he, "I could eat the hauf o't for a' the brose I hae suppit."

"Grip it," quo' the wife, "and I'll hae a bit too. Cast your breeks at it—kep—kep!"

The goodman cuist the breeks and had near-hand smoor't it, but it warsl't out and ran, and the goodman after't wantin' the breeks; and there was a clean chase owre the craft park and up the wunyerd, and in among the whins; and the goodman lost it and had to come his wa's trottin' hame hauf-nakit.

But now it was grown dark and the wee bunnock couldna see; but it gaed into the side o' a muckle whin bush and into a tod's hole. The tod had gotten nae meat for twa days.

"O welcome, welcome," quo' the tod, and snappit it in twa i' the middle. And that was the end o' the wee bunnock.

"Now weans, an ye live to grow muckle, be na ower lifted up aboot onything, nor owre sair cuisten down; for ye see the folk were a' cheated and the puir tod got the bunnock."

NOTES

1. When a boy was apprenticed to a tailor he sat cross-legged on a table, learning his trade. An old man in Selkirk, talking of Tom Scott, R.S.A., with whom he had grown up, used to tell how "his faither ettled to put him on the board".
2. The fire being in the middle of the floor.
3. A slightly rueful gibe at the miller. Thanks to the thirlage laws he never lacked custom, so his sowens were not likely to be thin.

The Marriage of Robin Redbreast

Place: Ayrshire.
Source: Robert Chambers, *Popular Rhymes of Scotland.*
Narrator: Mrs. Begg, sister of Robert Burns.

"The poet was in the habit of telling it to the younger members of his father's household, and Mrs. Begg's impression is that he *made* it for their amusement."

It is pleasant to know that Robert Chambers gave the entire profits of a cheap edition of his *Life and Works of Burns* to Mrs. Begg.

There was an auld gray Poussie Baudrons and she gaed awa' doon by a water-side, and there she saw a wee Robin Redbreast happin' on a brier; and Poussie Baudrons says: "Where's tu gaun, wee Robin?" And wee Robin says: "I'm gaun awa' to the king to sing him a sang this guid Yule morning."

And Poussie Baudrons says: "Come here, wee Robin, and I'll let you see a bonny white ring round my neck." But wee Robin says: "Na, na! gray Poussie Baudrons, na, na! Ye worry't the wee mousie, but ye'se no worry me."

So wee Robin flew awa' till he came to a fail fauld-dike and there he saw a gray greedy gled sitting. And gray greedy gled says: "Where's tu gaun, wee Robin?" And wee Robin says: "I'm gaun awa' to the king to sing him a song this guid Yule morning."

And gray greedy gled says: "Come here, wee Robin, and I'll let ye see a bonny feather in my wing." But wee Robin says: "Na, na! gray greedy gled, na, na! Ye pookit a' the wee lintie, but ye'se no pook me."

So wee Robin flew awa' till he came to the cleugh o' a craig, and there he saw slee Tod Lowrie sitting. And slee Tod Lowrie says: "Where's tu gaun, wee Robin?" And wee Robin says; "I'm gaun awa' to the king to sing him a sang this guid Yule morning."

And slee Tod Lowrie says: "Come here, wee Robin, and I'll let ye see a bonny spot on the tap o' my tail." But wee Robin says: "Na, na! slee Tod Lowrie; na, na! Ye worry't the wee lammie, but ye'se no worry me."

So wee Robin flew awa' till he came to a bonny burnside, and there he saw a wee callant sitting. And the wee callant says: "Where's tu gaun, wee Robin?" And wee Robin says, "I'm gaun awa' to the king to sing him a sang this guid Yule morning."

And the wee callant says: "Come here, wee Robin, and I'll gie ye a wheen grand moolins out o' my pooch." But wee Robin says: "Na, na! wee callant; na, na! Ye speldert the gowdspink, but ye'se no spelder me."

So wee Robin flew awa' till he cam' to the king, and there he sat on a winnock-sole and sang the king a bonny sang. And the king says to the queen: "What'll we gie to wee Robin for singing us this bonny song?"

And the queen says to the king: "I think we'll gie him the wee wran to be his wife.

So wee Robin and the wee wran were married, and the king and the queen and a' the court danced at the waddin'; syne he flew awa' hame to his ain water-side, and happit on a brier.

The Wee Wifie and her Coggie

Place: Aberdeenshire.
Source: *Scottish Notes and Queries.*

"A tale well known to the young of some sixty years ago;" (i.e. in the early nineteenth century) "told before the peat fire on winter evenings, often repeated and always attentively listened to."

There wiz a wee wifie wha dwalt at the fit o' a hill. She had bit ae coggie, an' she washed it clean, clean, an' set it out on the dyke to dry; an' whan the wifie ga'ed in tae her hoosie the coggie jumpit doon aff the dyke an gaed loupin' awa'

> O'er hills and o'er happocks,
> O'er cairns and o'er knapocks

till it cam' to a wee mannie diggin' gowd.

"Fair fa' yer bonnie face," said the wee mannie, "whaur come ye frae?"

"I come frae the wee wifie at the fit o' the hill; she washed me clean and set me oot to dry."

"Weel," said the mannie, "gin ye wad gang to the fit o' the far awa' hill an' bring me frae the bonnie spring there a drink o' pure spring water, ye sall hae yer reward."

Syne the coggie gaed loupin' awa' again,

> O'er hills and o'er happocks,
> O'er cairns and o'er knapocks

till it cam' to the bonnie spring at the fit o' the far awa' hill. There it dipped in three times an' cam' up lipperin' fu', syne back again to the mannie diggin' gowd.

"Ma blessin' on ye," said the mannie, "ye're a guid servator. Ye sall hae yer reward."

An' he took the coggie up an' drank it toom, an syne filled it wi' twa gowpens o' gowd, saying, "that's for the wee wifie that washed ye clean. Haste ye hame afore the nicht fa', an' gie her ma thanks."

An' the coggie set aff hame

> O'er hills and o'er happocks
> O'er cairns and o'er knapocks

till it got back to the wee hoosie at the fit o' the hill an' syne jumpit up on the dyke. An' whan the wifie cam' oot to tak' in her coggie she gat it fu' o' gowd, an' never mair kent want as lang as she leeved.

Jock and his Mother[1]

Place: Lowlands generally.
Source: Robert Chambers, *Popular Rhymes of Scotland*.
Collector: Andrew Henderson.

There was a wife that had a son, and they ca'd him Jock; and she said to him:

"You're a lazy fallow! Ye maun gang awa' and do something for to help me."

"Weel," says Jock, "I'll do that."

So awa' he gangs, and fa's in wi' a packman. Says the packman: "If ye carry my pack a' day, I'll gie ye a needle at night."

So he carried the pack, and got the needle; and as he was gaun awa' hame to his mither, he cuts a burden o' brackens, and put the needle into the heart o' them. Awa' he gaes hame. Says his mither: "What hae ye made o' yersel the day?"

Says Jock, "I fell in wi' a packman, and carried his pack a' day and he ga'e me a needle for't; and ye may look for it amang the brackens."

"Hout," quo' she, "ye daft gowk, ye should hae stuck it into your bonnet, man."

"I'll mind that again," quo' Jock.

Next day he fell in wi' a man carrying plough socks.

"If ye help me to carry my socks a' day, I'll gie ye ane tae yersel' at night."

"I'll do that," quo' Jock.

Jock carries them a' day, and gets a sock which he sticks in his bonnet. On the way hame he was dry, and gaed awa' to tak a drink out o' the burn, and wi' the weight o' the sock it fell into the water and gaed out o' sight. He gaed hame, and his mother says; "Weel, Jock, what hae ye been doing a' day?" And then he tells her.

"Hout," quo' she, "ye should hae tied a string to it and trailed it behind you."

"Weel," quo' Jock, "I'll mind that again."

Awa' he sets and he fa's in wi' a flesher.

"Weel," says the flesher, "if ye'll be my servant a' day I'll gie ye a leg o' mutton at night."

"I'll be that," quo' Jock. So he gets his leg o' mutton at night; he ties a string to it and trails it behind him the hale road hame.

"What hae ye been doing?" says his mither. He tells her. "Hout, ye fool, ye should hae carried it on your shouther."

"I'll mind that again," quo' Jock.

"Awa' he goes next day, and meets a horse-dealer. He says, "If ye will help me wi' my horses a' day, I'll gie ye ane tae yersel' at night."

"I'll do that," quo' Jock. So he served him and got his horse and he ties its feet and carries it on his shouther.

"Hout ye daft gowk," says his mither, "ye'll ne'r turn wise! Could ye no hae loupen on it and ridden it?"

"I'll mind that agin," quo' Jock.

Aweel, there was a grand gentleman who had a daughter wha was very subject to melancholy. Her father gave out that whaever should make her laugh would get her in marriage. So it happened that she was sitting at the window musing in her melancholy state, when Jock cam by wi' the horse on his shouther. And she burst into a fit o' laughter. When they asked what made her laugh it was found to be Jock, and so Jock was sent for to get his bride.

Weel, Jock was married to her and there was a great supper. Amongst other things there was some honey, which Jock was very fond o'. After supper they were bedded and the auld priest[2] that married them sat up a' night by the fireside. Jock wakens in the night and says, "O wad ye gic me some o' yon nice sweet honey that we got to our supper?"

"O ay," says his wife; "rise and gang into the press and ye'll get a pig fou o't."

Jock rises and thrusts his hand into the honey-pig for a nievefu', and he could not get it out. So he cam awa' wi' the pig on his hand, like a mason's mell, and says: "Oh, I canna get my hand oot."

"Hout," quo' she, "gang awa' and break it on the cheek-stane."[3]

By this time the fire was dark, and the auld priest was lying snoring wi' his head against the chimney-piece, wi' a huge white wig on. Jock gaes awa' and ga'e him a whack wi' the honey-pig on the head, thinking it was the cheek-stane. The auld priest roars out "Murder!" Jock tak's down the stair as hard as he can bicker, and hides himsel' amang the bees'-skeps.

That night, as luck wad have it, some thieves came to steal the bees'-skeps and in the hurry o' tumbling them into a large grey plaid they tumbled Jock in alang wi' them. So aff they set wi' Jock and the skeps on their backs. On the way they had to cross the burn where Jock had lost his bannet. Ane o' the thieves cries, "O I hae fand a bannet!" and Jock, hearing this, cries out "Oh, that's mine!"

They thocht they had the deil on their backs, so they let a' fa' in the burn, and Jock, being tied in the plaid couldna get out; so he and the bees were a' drowned thegither.

And if a' tales be true, that's nae lee.

NOTES

1. "Numskull" tales were extremely popular and are of very ancient origin. Many of them came to Scotland from the Baltic seaboard.
2. Priest. This may date the story before the Reformation, or indicate its origin in a predominantly Catholic area.
3. Cheek-stane. See note 5 to "Working Stones in the Days of the Tales", p. 149.

The Clever Apprentice

Place: Banff.
Source: *Folklore Journal*, vol. 7, 1889.
Collector: The Rev. Walter Gregor.

A shoemaker once employed an apprentice.

"What would you call me when you speak to me?" he asked.

"I would call you master," said the boy.

"No," said the shoemaker, "you must call me Master of all Masters. What would you call my trousers?"

"Oh, I would just call them trousers."

"No, you must call them struntifers. What would you call my wife?"

"I would call her Mistress."

"No, you must call her the fair Lady Permoumadam. And what would you call my son?"

"I would call him Johnny."

"No, you must call him John the Great. What would you call the cat?"

"I would just call him Pussy."

"No, you must call him Great Carle Gropius.[1] What would you call the fire?"

"Oh I would call it fire."

"No, you must call it Fire Evangelist. And the peatstack?"

"I would call that the peatstack."

"No, you must call it Mount Potago. What would you call the well?"

"I would just call it the well."

"No, you must call it the Fair Fountain. Last of all, what would you call the house?"

"I would call it the house."

"No, you must call it the Castle of Mungo."

Then the shoemaker told the lad that the first time he had occasion to use all these words at once his apprenticeship would be at an end.

The apprentice was not long in making an occasion. One morning he got up early and lit the fire. Then he tied papers to the cat's tail and threw him into the fire. The cat ran out with the blazing papers, landed in the peatstack and set it on fire.

"Master of all Masters," shouted the apprentice, "start up and jump into your strontifers, and call upon John the Great and the fair Lady Permoumadam, for the Great Carle Gropius has got hold of Fire Evangelist and he's out to Mount Potago, and if you don't get help from the Fair Fountain the whole of Castle Mungo will burn to the ground."

And that was the end of the apprenticeship.

NOTE

1. Carle Gropius was the name of a bugbear which kept children quiet. It was also the contemptuous term for a stupid man, cf. Meister Grobian of German literature.

Mally Whuppie[1]

Place: Aberdeenshire.
Source: *Folklore Journal,* vol. 4, 1884.
Narrator: Mrs. Moir of Old Meldrum.
Collector: The Rev. Walter Gregor.

Once upon a time there was a man and his wife had too many children and they could not get meat for them, so they took the three youngest and left them in a wood.

They travelled and travelled and could never see a house. It began to be dark and they were hungry. At last they saw a light and made for it, and it turned out to be a house. They knocked at the door and a woman came to it and asked them what they wanted. They said if she could let them in and gie them a piece. The woman said she could not do that as her man was a giant and he would fell them if he came home. They priggit that she would let them stop for a little whilie and they would go away before he came. So she took them in an set them doon afore the fire, and gave them milk and breid; but just as they had begun to eat, a great knock came to the door and a dreadful voice said:

"Fee, fie, fo, fum,
I smell the blood of some earthly one.

Who have you there, wife?"

"Eh," said the wife, "its three peer lassies caul' an hungry, an they will go away. Ye winna touch them, man."

He said nothing, but ate up a great big supper, and ordered them to stay the night. Now he had three lassies of his own, and they were to sleep in the same bed with the three strangers. The youngest of the three strange lassies was called Mally Whuppie, and she was very clever. She noticed that before they went to bed the giant put straw rapes round her neck and her sisters', and round his ain lassies' necks he put gold chains. So Mally took care and didn't fall asleep but waited until she was sure everyone else was sleeping sound. Then she slippit oot o' the bed and took the straw rapes off her own and her sisters' necks, and took the gold chains off the giant's lassies. She put the straw rapes on the giant's lassies and the gold on herself and her sisters, and lay down.

In the middle of the night up rose the giant armed with a great club and felt for the necks with the straw. It was dark. He took his own lassies out on the floor and laid upon them till they were dead, and then lay down again thinking he had managed fine.

Mally thought it time she and her sisters were out of that, so she wakened them and told them to be quiet and they slippit out of the house and they ran and ran and never stoppit till morning, when they saw a great house before them. It turned out to be a king's house; so Mally went in and told her story to the king.

He said, "Well, Mally, you're a clever cutty and you've managed well; but if you would manage better and go back and steal the giant's sword that hangs on the back of his bed, I would give your eldest sister my eldest son to marry."

Mally said she would try. So she went back and managed to slip into the giant's house and crept in below his bed. The giant came home and ate up a great supper and went to bed. Mally waited until he was snoring, then she crept out and raxed in ower the giant and got down the sword; but just as she got it oot ower the bed it gave a rattle, and up jumped the giant, and Mally oot at the door and the sword with her; and she ran and he ran, till they came to the Brig o' ae Hair[2] an' she won ower, but he cudna, and he says: "Wae worth you, Mally Whuppie! lat ye never come again." And she says, "Twice yet, carle," quo' she, "I'll come to Spain."

So Mally took the sword to the king and her sister was married to his son.

Well, the king he says: "Ye've managed well, Mally; but if ye would manage better and steal the purse that's below the giant's pillow, I would marry your second sister to my second son." And Mally says she would try.

So she set out for the giant's house and slippit in and hid again below the bed and waited till the giant had finished his supper and was snoring sound asleep. She slippit oot and slippit her hand below the pillow and got out the purse, but just as she was going out the giant wakened and after her; and she ran and he ran till they cam to the Brig o' ae Hair, and she won ower, but he cudna, and he said, "Wae worth you, Mally Whuppie! lat ye never come again." And she said, "Aince yet, carle," quo' she, "I'll come to Spain."

I

So Mally took the purse to the king and her second sister was married to the king's second son.

After that the king says, "Mally, you're a clever cutty, but if you would dae better yet and steal the giant's ring off his finger, I'll give you my youngest son to yourself." And Mally said she would try.

So back she goes to the giant's house and hides herself below the bed. The giant wisna lang ere he cam hame, and after he had eaten a great big supper he went to his bed and soon was snoring loud. Mally crept out and raxed in ower the bed and got hold of the giant's hand, and she pult and pult till she got off the ring; but just as she got it off the giant got up and grippit her by the hand, and he says, "Now I hae catcht you, Mally Whuppie, and if I had deen as muckle ill to you as you hae deen to me, what wad ye dae to me?"

Mally considered what plan she would fall upon to escape, and she says, "I wad pit you into a pyock, and I wad pit the cat in aside you and the dog in aside you, and a needle and a thread and shears; and I wad hang you up upon the wa', and I wad gang to the wood and wale the thickest stick I could get, and I would come hame and take you down and lay upon you till you were dead."

"Well, Mally," says the giant, "I'll just do that to you."

So he gets a pyock and puts Mally into it, and the cat and the dog beside her, and a needle and thread and shears, and hings her up upon the wa' and goes to the wood to choose a stick.

Mally she sings, "Oh gin ye saw fhat I see! Oh gin ye saw fhat I see!"

"Oh," says the giant's wife, "fhat divv ye see, Mally?"

But Mally never said a word but, "Oh, gin ye saw fhat I see!"

The giant's wife pleaded that Mally wad tak her up into the pyock till she wad see what Mally saw. So Mally took the shears and cut a hole in the pyock, and took the needle and thread with her. She jumpit doon and helpit the giant's wife up, and sewed up the hole in the pyock.

The giant's wife saw nothing, and began to ask to get down again. Mally never minded, but hid herself at the back of the door. Home came the giant, and a great big tree in his hand. He took down the pyock and began to lay upon it.

His wife cried, "It's me, man, it's me!" But the dog barkit and the cat mewt and he did not know his wife's voice. But Mally did not want her to be killed,[3] so she came out from the back of the door.

The giant saw her and he after her, and she ran and he ran till they cam to the Brig o' ae Hair, and she wan ower but he cudna; and he said, "Wae worth you, Mally Whuppie! Lat ye never come again."

"Never mair, carle," quo' she, "will I come again to Spain."

So Mally Whuppie took the ring to the king, and she was married to his youngest son, and she never saw the giant again.

NOTES

1. This is one of the tales that crossed the Highland Line on the far side of which it was known as Maol a Chliobain. J. F. Campbell collected it in Islay and versions have been found in Norway, Iceland, Germany, Denmark and Ireland. By the time it reached Old Meldrum its character had changed—Mally Whuppie is a much kindlier creature than the grim Maol a Chliobain.

2. A bridge as fine as a hair is a very old and important motif in folklore. The Norse gods had a bridge to heaven over which giants could not pass, and the Moslem paradise is approached by a bridge as fine as a hair. Mally's bridge may have been a rainbow.

   The sword is also an ancient and significant motif. The rattle of the giant's sword is a feeble echo of the voice of the Glaive of Light of Celtic mythology, which was a personage as well as a weapon.

3. Maol a Chliobain had no such human feelings.

The Strange Visitor

Place: Lowlands generally.
Source: Robert Chambers, *Popular Rhymes of Scotland.*

A great favourite with Scottish children, although the figure is that of death. "The dialogue, towards the end, is managed in a low drawling manner so as to rivet the attention and awaken an undefined awe in the juvenile audience. Thus wrought up, the concluding words come upon them with such effect as generally to cause a scream of alarm."

A wife was sitting at her reel ae night;
    And aye she sat, and aye she reeled, and aye she wished for
    company.

In came a pair of braid braid soles, and sat down at the fireside;
    And aye she sat, and aye she reeled, and aye she wished for
    company.

In came a pair o' sma' sma' legs, and sat down on the braid braid
    soles;
    And aye she sat, and aye she reeled, and aye she wished for
    company.

In came a pair o' muckle muckle knees, and sat down on the sma'
    sma' legs;
    And aye she sat, and aye she reeled, and aye she wished for
    company.

In came a pair o' sma' sma' thees, and sat down on the muckle
    muckle knees;
    And aye she sat, and aye she reeled, and aye she wished for
    company.

In came a pair o' muckle muckle hips, and sat down on the sma'
    sma' thees;
    And aye she sat, and aye she reeled, and aye she wished for
    company.

In came a sma' sma' waist, and sat down on the muckle muckle
    hips;
    And aye she sat, and aye she reeled, and aye she wished for
    company.

In came a pair o' braid braid shouthers, and sat down on the
    sma' sma' waist;
    And aye she sat, and aye she reeled, and aye she wished for
    company.

In came a pair o' sma' sma' arms, and sat down on the braid
    braid shouthers;
    And aye she sat, and aye she reeled, and aye she wished for
    company.

In came a pair o' muckle muckle hands, and sat down on the sma'
 sma' arms;
  And aye she sat, and aye she reeled, and aye she wished for
  company.

In came a sma' sma' neck, and sat down on the braid braid
  shouthers.
  And aye she sat, and aye she reeled, and aye she wished for
  company.

In came a great big head, and sat down on the sma' sma' neck.

"What way hae ye sic braid braid feet?" quo the wife.
"Muckle ganging, muckle ganging" (*gruffly*)
"What way hae ye sic sma' sma' legs?"
"Aih-h-h—late—and wee-e-e moul" (*whiningly*)

"What way hae ye sic muckle muckle knees?"
"Muckle praying, muckle praying" (*piously*)
"What way hae ye sic sma' sma' thees?"
"Aih-h-h—late—and we-e-e—moul"

"What way hae ye sic big big hips?"
"Muckle sitting, muckle sitting"
"What way hae ye sic a sma' sma' waist?"
"Aih-h-h—late—and wee-e-e—moul."

"What way hae ye sic braid braid shouthers?"
"Wi' carrying broom, wi' carrying broom,"
"What way hae ye sic sma' sma' arms?"
"Aih-h-h—late—and wee-e-e moul."

"What way hae ye sic muckle muckle hands?"
"Threshing wi' an iron flail, threshing wi' an iron flail."
"What way hae ye sic a sma' sma' neck?"
"Aih-h-h—late—and wee-e-e—moul."

"What way hae ye sic a muckle, muckle head?"
"Muckle wit, muckle wit."
"What do ye come for?"
"FOR YOU!"

Self

Place: North of Scotland generally.
Source: *Folklore Journal.* "A never failing source of merriment
when told to a group of young children."

There was once a miller that missed a quantity of his meal every
morning and he decided to sit up one night and watch. At
twelve o'clock he saw a wee man coming into the mill and filling
his cappie wi' the meal, so he asked what he was and what was
his name.

The wee man said his name was Self, and asked what the
miller's name was.

"I'm Self too," said the miller, and struck the wee man with a
big stick, which made him roar.

An old woman came running, crying, "Wha did it? Wha did
it?"

"Self did it," said the miller, and she gave *him* a smack on the
side of the head, saying, "If Self did it Self must mend it."

VI

THE FAIRIES' FAREWELL

ABOUT the year 1850 a Galloway roadman refused point-blank to obey the County Council's order to widen the highway at a certain point between Glenluce and Newton Stewart by cutting down an ancient thorn reputed to be fairy property. Authority was tolerant, and the tree remained, standing well out on the road and impeding traffic for another seventy years, a witness to the fear of uncanny reprisals.[1]

But Galloway was exceptional. In less isolated parts of the Lowlands the fairies' day was done by the late eighteenth century. Brooding on their disappearance, an old woman came to the regretful conclusion that "there was sae much preaching, and folk reading the Bible that they got frichted", and no doubt this was one reason, though the Reformation seems scarcely to have daunted them—witness their attempt to infiltrate the Kirk Session of Borgue. It was with the agricultural revolution that the hour struck: their dancing rings ploughed, their green hills sown with grain, their existence not so much denied as ignored.

> Where the scythe cuts and the sock rives
> Hae done wi' fairies and bee bykes . . .

It was total defeat; and yet the fairies contrived to surrender on their own terms, staging a ceremonial departure, widely observed and pinned firmly to the margin of history by a date which—apart from Galloway—is roughly the same throughout Scotland. Whatever took place, or was imagined, round about the year 1790, descriptions of it recorded as far apart as Nithsdale and Caithness are detailed, vivid and surprisingly alike. Invested with a curious atmosphere of mystery and regret, it is known as the Fairies' Farewell.

NOTE

1. This thorn was believed to cure toothache. The sufferer probed the sore tooth with a wooden pin which was then driven into the tree, after which the pain duly ceased. See *Transactions of the Naturalist and Antiquarian Society of Dumfries and Galloway*, 1912-13.

Farewell to the People of Peace

Place: Cromarty.
Source: Hugh Miller, *Old Red Sandstone* (Note to chapter XI).

On a Sabbath morning nearly sixty years ago, the inmates of a hamlet close to a ravine had all gone to church except for a herd boy and his little sister. Just as the shadow of the garden-dial had fallen on the line of noon, they saw a long cavalcade ascending out of the ravine. . . . The horses were shaggy diminutive things, speckled dun and grey; the riders stunted, misgrown, ugly creatures, attired in antique jerkins of plaid, long grey cloaks and little red caps from under which their long uncombed locks shot out over their cheeks and foreheads.

The boy and his sister stood gazing in utter dismay and astonishment as rider after rider, each one more uncouth and dwarfish than the one that had preceded it, passed and disappeared among the brushwood that covered the hill until at length the entire route, except the last rider, had gone by.

"What are ye, little mannie? And where are ye going?" enquired the boy.

"Not of the race of Adam," said the creature, turning for a moment in his saddle. "The People of Peace shall never more be seen in Scotland."

Farewell to the Burrow Hill

Place: Nithsdale.
Source: R. H. Cromek, *Remains of Galloway and Nithsdale Song.*
Collector: Allan Cunningham.
    "The Fairy Farewell is a circumstance that happened about twenty years ago and is well remembered." This puts the incident at about 1790.

The sun was setting on a fine summer's evening and the peasantry were returning from their labour when, on the side of a green hill, appeared a procession of, apparently, little boys habited in mantles of green, freckled with light. One, taller than the rest, ran before them and seemed to enter the hill, and again appeared at its summit.

This was repeated three times, and all vanished. The people who beheld it called it "The Fareweel o' the Fairies to the Burrow Hill".

The Forsaken Fairy

Place: Borders.
Source: Sir George Douglas, *Scottish Fairy and Folk Tales.*
Narrator: Robert Oliver, a shepherd on Jed Water who died about 1820.

I can tell ye about the vera last fairy that was seen hereaway.

When my faither was a young man he lived at Hyndlee an' herdit the Brocklaw. Weel, it was the custom to milk the yowes in thae days, an' my faither was buchtin' the Brocklaw yowes to twae young, lish, clever hizzies ae nicht i' the gloamin'. Nae little gabbin' an' daffin' gaed on amang the threesome, I'se warrant ye, till at last, just as it chanced to get darkish, my faither chancit to luik alang the lea at the head o' the bucht, an' what did he see but a wee little creaturie a' clad i' green, an' wi' lang hair, yellow as gowd, hingin' round its shoulders, comin' straight for him, whiles gi'en a whink o' a greet, an' aye atween its haunds raisin' a queer, unyirthly cry, 'Hae ye seen Hewie Milburn? Oh! hae ye seen Hewie Milburn?'

Instead o' answering the creature, my faither sprang ower the bucht-flake to be near the lasses, saying "Bliss us a'—what's that?"

"Ha, ha! Patie lad," quo Bessie Elliot, a free-spoken Liddesdale hempy; "theer a wife com'd for ye the nicht, Patie lad."

"A wife!" said my faither. "May the Lord keep me frac sic a wife as that!" and he confessed till his deein' day he was in sic a fear that the hairs o' his heid stuid up like the birses of a hurcheon.

The creature was nae bigger than a three-year-auld lassie, but feat an' tight, lithe o' limb as ony grown woman, an' its face was the doonright perfection o' beauty, only there was something wild and unyirthly in its e'en that couldna be lookit at, faur less describit: it didna molest them, but aye taigl't on aboot the bucht, now and then repeatin' its cry, "Hae ye seen Hewie Milburn?" Sae they cam' to nae ither conclusion than that it had tint its companion.

When my faither and the lasses left the bucht it followed them hame to the Hyndlee kitchen, where they offered it yowe brose, but it wadna tak' onything till at last a ne'er-do-weel callant made as if he wad grip it wi' a pair o' reed-het tangs, an' it appeared to be offendit, an' gaed awa' doon the burnside, cryin' its auld cry eerier an' waesomer than ever, and disappeared in a bush o' seggs.

VII

THE SAINTS TAKE OVER

HOWEVER severe the official attitude, the line between religion and folklore was not entirely rigid. A certain amount of give and take went quietly on. It was rather abortive on the giving side: St. Brendan failed to persuade an inquiring mermaid into the fold, and there is no record that Rome itself had any better success with the goblin despatched for its attention by St. Fillan. But the taking process went steadily on, first as the ancient magic symbols were adapted by the Church, bent on easing the pagan world into Christianity, and later by monks appointed to write the lives of the Saints.

Their labours were inspired by a sort of inter-house rivalry, each Foundation determined that its own revered holy man should dazzle the eyes of the world with signs and wonders. Zeal and devotion often outran accuracy. It was the spirit of the thing that mattered; and if the monastic archives or oral tradition failed to equip a particular saint with enough miraculous stories they had to be borrowed, usually from some source within the Church, but if the worst came to the worst from the vast resources of folklore—"the hotch-potch of material from popular tales".[1]

So we find, neatly fitted into a twelfth-century life of St. Kentigern, a miracle which can be traced back through Irish folklore (St. Bride also borrowed it) and heroic romance to ancient Arabic times. With appropriate touches of local colour it settled down so well that eventually it stole the Kentigern picture, displacing the "accredited" miracles and perpetuating itself on the arms of Glasgow.

It is interesting to know that "it can be gathered from references in the St. Mungo legends that there was once a sacred grove on the site occupied by Glasgow Cathedral . . . when he arrived, Glasgow was called *Cathures*. It has been suggested that this is a Latinized form of the Gaelic word 'cathair' [literally a chair], signifying in modern times 'fairy knoll'. Having taken over the holy place the Saint had attached to him the legends and beliefs associated with it. . . ."[2] Among these would be the salmon of knowledge and the magic gold ring.

The group of tales which follows belongs to a sort of debatable ground between folklore and hagiography.

NOTES

1. See N. H. Chadwick, *Studies in the Early British Church* ("The Sources for the Life of St. Kentigern", by K. H. Jackson).
2. See B643041, p. 54. Mitchell Library, Glasgow. Donald MacKenzie.

St. Kentigern and the Ring

Place: Glasgow and West of Scotland.
Source: William Stevenson, *Legends of St. Kentigern*. Taken
from the version of the monk David Camerius.

The Queen of Scotland possessed a certain ring of great value
which she had received from the king as a pledge of extreme
love; but by some accident she lost it while, whether by sea or by
land, she was visiting the royal palaces of the kingdom.

Observing, on her return home, that the ring was missing, the
king became suspicious and with some warmth demanded it of
her; but she, conscious of her conjugal fidelity, in grief and sad-
ness of heart turned to God urgently imploring of Him that in
his infinite goodness and clemency He would restore the lost ring
and have respect to her shame.

After her prayer, St. Kentigern came to the thoughts of the
Queen. Knowing that the holy bishop was celebrated for his
miracles, she went to him with many tears, imploring him to
protect her reputation and by the help of God, with Whom she
knew there was nothing impossible, to restore the lost ring. And
the holy servant of God, moved with compassion, told her to
hope the best.

The Saint then resorted to prayer, and the spirit of God came
upon him. Rising from his devotions, he betook himself with
rapid step to the river Clud, which abounds in salmon, and to
the first fisher he met he said, "Cast your net as speedily as
you can for a draught, and bring me alive the first fish you
catch."

Scarcely had the net been cast when lo! a large and solitary
salmon was caught by it, which, on being presented by the
fisherman, was accepted by the Saint. Having made the sign of
the Cross, he thrust his hand into the mouth of the fish and
pulling out the king's ring freely gave it to the Queen, who stood
by in astonishment at what she saw. The fish, which had been the
instrument of so great a service, he ordered to be restored to its
liberty in the river.

NOTE

1. The legend is a version of the tale of King Solomon's Ring, No. B. 5482 in Stith-Thomson's *Motif Index of Folk Lore*. It is widespread in Jewish and Arabic, as well as Gaelic folklore and is quoted by Herodotus.

In the better known version the King's suspicions are justified. He finds the Queen's lover asleep, takes the ring from his finger, throws it into the river and goes back to challenge the Queen. The saint takes pity on her and she confesses her fault. Dr. Stevenson's comment is: "The story lacked a Magdalen, for whom the story-telling monks of those times displayed an overwhelming predilection. So, at the expense of the Queen's reputation, this was supplied."

St. Mungo's Cheese

Place: West of Scotland.
Source: *The Aberdeen Breviary*, printed by Chepman in 1509, where it has the dignity of Latin:
    R. Vertitur in lapides mox compressi copia lactis Formatum prisca manet atque figura.
    V. Fons tenet aeternum liquidus per secula nomen.
Retold: William Stevenson, *Legends of St. Kentigern*.

A certain skilled artificer was employed by the man of God about the monastery and suitably remunerated. But the Saint was accustomed to use milk for both meat and drink, because he abstained from every kind of liquor by the which a man could be intoxicated. From his own stock of new milk, accordingly, he ordered two pitchersful to be conveyed to his artificer. But when the bearer was passing over the river Clyde the lids of the pitchers fell off and the whole of the milk was spilt in the water.

But—a marvellous and most unusual thing!—the spilt milk was in no degree mingled with the water or changed in respect of taste and colour. With incomprehensible rapidity it was turned into cheese, nor was the cheese less effectually consolidated by the beating of the waves than any other of this kind is wont to be by the compression of the hands.

The bearer snatched this well-shaped cheese from the water and gave it to the artificer.

St. Ninian and the Leeks

Place: Galloway.
Source: Aelred of Rievaux, *Life of St. Ninian*.
    (Aelred was educated in Scotland along with Prince Henry, son of David 1.)

It happened on a certain day that the holy man went with his brethren into the refectory to dine and seeing no pot-herbs or vegetables on the table he called the brother who was entrusted with the care of the garden and enquired why on that day no pot-herbs or vegetables were set before the brethren.

"Truly, O Father," he replied, "whatever remained of the leeks and such like, I today committed to the ground and the garden has not yet produced anything fit for eating."

Then said the Saint: "Go, and whatever thy hand findeth, gather and bring to me."

Amazed, he stood trembling, hesitating what to do. But knowing that Ninian could command nothing in vain, he went slowly to the garden. There happened a marvellous thing, credible to those alone who think that nothing is impossible to him that believeth; for he saw leeks and all other kinds of vegetables, not only grown but bearing seed. He was astonished, and as if in a trance thought he saw a vision.

At length, coming to himself and remembering the power of the holy man, he gave thanks to God, and gathering as many as seemed sufficient, he set them on the table before the bishop. The guests looked at each other, and with one heart and voice magnified God working in His saints, and so withdrew, refreshed much more in mind than in body.

NOTE

1. The original form, from which this was borrowed, is known as "Strawberries in Winter" (Stith-Thomson H. 1023.3). Also attributed to St. Kentigern in Jocelyn's *Life*, where the out-of-season fruit is the bramble. An early version of the tale follows, taken from an MS. in the University Library at Cambridge.

Sa a tyme can befal	(*did*)
That he among his brethire al	
Went to meet in the frature,	(*refectory*)
As he that of them had the cure,	(*care*)
To tak sic commone fude	
As thai did, il or gude,	

And saw the burdis thru the hale   (*boards*)
That service was nane of cale.
Then the monk that keping hade
Of the yard he callit but bade   (*without delay*)
And askit him quhy that thai
Were nocht servit of caile that day.
Then said he: "Faddir, but wene   (*without doubt*)
In the yarde is nane erbe grene."
And the Bishop, that suth wiste,   (*who knew Truth*)
Bad hyme pass furth but ony first (*without any delay*)
And quhat he in the yard fand
Bring til hyme in his hand.
And furth he went at bidding,
Tho he wiste weel to find na thing,
And in the yard soon has sene
Caile and leikis faire and grene,
And al that men of had neid,
Then cummyne of new sawine seide.
The monk that saw this ferly   (*miracle*)
Was then as in extasy,
Seand Niniane sa ful of grace
That gert that grow in sa little space.
Lofand God, therof tuk he
And brocht before them all to see.
And God thai lowit monyfald   (*praised*)
For this merwale, bath young and ald.

The Herd's Tale

Place: Galloway.
Source: *Gallovidian Annual*, No. xiv. "A tale of St. Ringan."
Narrator: Janet Tait, a field worker in the Stewartry.
Collector: Miss M. Dunn, great grand-daughter of Joseph Train.

Janet Tait heard the tale from her grandmother, born about 1746, to whom it had come from her great grandfather who claimed to have got it from the herd himself, as a very old man. This brings it into the category of a genuine folk tale, unlike the two previous stories.

K

When my grannie was a lassie her feyther used to tell her that when *his* grandfeyther was a wee laddie he kenned an auld, auld man whae had been a herd and whae had seen Sanct Ringan.[1]

He was nocht but a herd laddie when he seen him, an' he bided wi' the herd in a wee clay hoose. The callant was but a papist, ye ken, but for a' that he was a douce laddie, an' no ill-guidit.

There cam' a Yule-e'en when his maister bude to gang far awa' tae a Yule Fair, an' he says to the laddie, "Jamie, I'll hae to lippen on ye tae look efter the yowes an' see that they're a' gaithered in afore the mirk."

Sae the herd-laddie was left a' his lane in the wee clay hoose, an' afore the gloamin' aff he gaed to gaither in the yowes. He found them a' forbye ane; an' he lookit, but he found nor hide nor hair o't. By noo it was the mirk, and gey oorie it was for the laddie; but he was a bield callant, an' when he had bedded a' the ither yowes, oot he set to seek the lost ane.

He lookit an' he lookit till he was fell wearit an' fair disjaskit wi' rowmin' ower the mosses an' amang the brambles. When he got to his ain door and foond nae yowe there he was awfu' ill aboot it and that wearit he could hardly think to gang ootbye ony mair; but he was vexed for the puir yowe an' fear't his maister wad think he hadna' been mindfu'.

Sae he sat doon by the hearth-stane to think what he could dae next. Syne he minded o' Sanct Ringan an' hoo folk bude to gang to his Well to pray him to find what was lost (no kennin' ony better, puir bodies), an' he keekit roon' to see what he could offer to the Sanct. An' his e'en lichted on his supper, whilk was kail brose he had got nae time to sup, an', says he, "I'm gey toom, but there's nocht else, so I'll e'en gie my supper to the Sanct."

Sae he picked up the bowl and gaed ower the brae to Sanct Ringan's Well and laid his supper doon on the well-stane. An' he kneeled doon an', says he: "O michty Sanct Ringan, I'm sair wearit an' I doot the yowe's awa', but gin ye can sup brose ye're welcome to mine, for it's a' that I hae."

He took a lang pech, an' he waitit an' waitit, but nocht cam' in view. By this time it was near twal' o' the clock, an' he thocht he wad seek doon to the moss ance mair; but afore he had gane faur frae the well he heard a chap on the well-stane ahint him, an' when he turned roon', here was a fremyt man in tattered claes suppin' the brose.

Says Jamie tae himsel', "Yon's nae Sanct; I ne'er heard tell o' a Sanct that wasna better puit-on. But, puir soul, he's hungry-like an' he'll maybe think mair o' the brose than ony Sanct wad dae."

Then says the man, wavin' the spun, "A fair gude-e'en to ye, my laddie."

"Fair gude-e'en," says Jamie. "It's no fair gude-e'en, nor fair gude-day wi' me, for I hae lost an auld yowe that my maister lippened on me to gaither in."

"Hoots," says the fremyt man, "the yowe's no sae faur awa'. Ye'll find her in a bramble bush in yon deep dyke ablow the saugh-trees that aye bud the sunest ilk spring."

"I hae socht her frae end to end o' yon dyke hauf a dizzen times the nicht," says the callant, fair pit oot at sic havers, "an she's no there."

But for a' that, the tap an' tail o't was, he went back to the dyke wi' the fremyt man, an' there ablow the busk was the yowe, no deid, but cam' ower dwammy wi' the cauld blast.

"I'm muckle obleeged to ye," says Jamie, "but I doot I'll no get her hame."

"Nae fear for that, " says the fremyt man, an' wi' that he happit her up on his shouder an' carried her hame to the fireside o' the wee clay hoose.

"It's fell dark," says the herd laddie, "Wull ye no bide the nicht wi' me?"

"I mauna dae that," says the fremyt man, "or I'll be late."

"Late?" says the callant, "An whaur may ye be gaun?"

The fremyt man was on the door-step an' he lookit back wi' a queer glint in his e'e. "Whaur wad I gang this nicht," says he "but to Bethlehem?"

An' wi' that he was awa', an' when the laddie rin to the door there was nae man to be seen, nocht but a bricht, glistenin' pathway to the East, for Sanct Ringan had walked that airt.

NOTE

1. Ringan was the Scots form of Ninian. Hence the name for the herb, Southernwood, connected with the Saint and traditionally carried to church between the leaves of bibles. Appelez Ringan—pray to Ringan —became first Apleringan, then Appleringie.

VIII

THE LAST ACT

LATE in the nineteenth century a secret was entrusted to a small boy
and his sister by an old couple who lived at Torrin, in Skye. The
old folk had guarded it until the last moment when the husband was
bedfast and the wife very frail, though still afoot. One summer
evening she beckoned to the children and, without a word, led them
away from her cottage over a range of low green hillocks towards the
setting sun.

Hillock after hillock they crossed, the old woman singing all the
time and the children following with a queer sense of compulsion.
Just at sunset they reached the farthest hillock where the grass parted
and . . . the fairy people came out.

The whole experience was so strange that brother and sister went
home in silence. It was not until next morning that they felt able to
compare notes; but they agreed then as to what they had seen.

The boy grew up to become a minister of the Church of Scotland
and—still with a sense of compulsion—put the incident on record in
the year 1967.

It seems only fitting that this last act should be left, without comment, to the fairies.

IX

APPENDIX
Some Collectors of the Tales

WITH few exceptions,[1] we owe nothing but gratitude to the men who collected the tales. Scott's description of Leyden bringing home the spoil is still warm with characteristic enthusiasm: "A sound was heard in the distance like that of the whistling of a tempest through the torn rigging of the vessel which scuds before it. The sounds increased, and "Leyden burst into the room chanting [the lost verses of] the ballad. He had walked between forty and fifty miles and back again for the sole purpose of visiting an old person who possessed this precious remnant of antiquity."[2]

NOTES

1. One of these exceptions, unfortunately, was Scott's own protégé Mr. Wilkie of Bowden (see below). Another was the Reverend William Stevenson, who chose to re-tell the Legends of St. Kentigern in somewhat flatulent prose; but they are the only complete versions which we possess.

2. Essay on Leyden. *Edinburgh Annual Register*, 1811.

JOSEPH TRAIN

In the spring of 1816 Sir Walter Scott sent an invitation to Joseph Train, Galloway exciseman and self-taught antiquarian, whom he knew only by correspondence:

I find I will be at my Farm of Abbotsford for a month, then in Town, and shall be glad to make your personal acquaintance.

The resulting visit was a very happy one for all concerned, but its great moment came unexpectedly and bore important fruit. A portrait of Claverhouse caught Train's eye as he and his host awaited breakfast in the study.

"Much more mild and gentle than one could suppose," he suggested, studying the features.

"Traduced by his Historians!" Scott was emphatic. He began to elaborate the theme with shrewd, vivid talk which brought the portrait to life.

"Why not a novel on this subject?" Train broke in at last; "and"—the idea suddenly expanded—"if the story was delivered as from the mouth of Old Mortality . . ."

"Old Mortality?" Scott snatched at the name, his voice harsh with excitement. "Man! *Who was he?*"

Information was eagerly supplied, and the great novel began to unfold.

This was by no means the first time Joseph Train had sown a seed in that fertile brain. Perhaps more than any other contemporary he understood and shared Scott's passion for the traditions of their country. According to his biographer (a son of Old Mortality himself) there was scarcely a ruin or cairn in the land he had failed to examine, or a fleeting fragment of tradition he had not gathered up. All his leisure was spent in this pursuit and his daily work continued it, taking him into the wilds of Galloway and Carrick where old customs and memories lingered. It was there he met Alexander McCreadie, then in his hundred and sixth year, still able to walk fourteen miles at a stretch, cook his own food, read the Psalms without spectacles and give a lucid account of rural life at the beginning of the eighteenth century.[1]

Travelling up to seven thousand miles in the course of a year—his annual salary for this was £200—Train was often storm-stayed in remote cottages where strange tales were told. Relics fell into his hands. He met queer characters. Beggars came to his door with ballads and old stories. He could have made a name for himself among scholars, but his ambition was to be of use to his "revered Sir Walter". Most of his relics went to Abbotsford and can still be seen in the museum there, but far more valuable was the steady flow of antiquarian material he sent to Scott over the years. Without it the Waverley Novels would have lacked Edie Ochiltree and Madge Wildfire, while *Guy Mannering* and *Wandering Willie's Tale* might never have been written.

Scott warmly acknowledged his debt to Train, but Scotland has never wakened up to the importance of this unassuming and unselfish scholar. His correspondence with Sir Walter can be found in the Manuscript Room of the National Library of Scotland, along with a battered notebook containing, among other matters, a full account of that significant visit to Castle Street, not omitting the main dish at the dinner-party held in his honour or a glimpse of the family breakfast next morning, attended by chattering children and hopeful dogs. One is glad to know that many more visits followed.

Scott's death left a permanent blank in Train's life, but nothing could diminish his antiquarian zeal. Study and collecting went on for another twenty years and the last picture shows "a tall old man with autumnal red in his face, hale-looking and of simple, quaint manners", the little parlour of his cottage near Castle Douglas full of rare antiquities. One of these, a magnificent piece of carving on black oak rescued from the ruins of Threave Castle, is one of the treasures in the Edinburgh Museum of Antiquities.

NOTE

1. In McCreadie's childhood the fields were still ploughed by oxen, ten in a yoke. Horses, when first used, were yoked four abreast and led from the front by a gaudman, walking backwards. There were no wheeled carts in his part of Galloway.

   He had no good word for his neighbour Col. Agnew of Shewchan, who had introduced into Galloway that "thriftless thing called a hat" in place of the Ayrshire bonnet.

ALLAN CUNNINGHAM

He was born in Nithsdale in 1784, his family "honest millers", time out of mind, though one of them had also served as an officer under Montrose. He left school at the age of eleven to train as a stone mason and in his spare time he enjoyed himself. Six foot in height, good-looking, a wide reader, an aspiring poet, he threw himself into any social life he could find and emerged quickly from obscurity. Before he was forty "all men of genius of the day, Scott, Wordsworth, Wilkie, Irving etc. are pleased with the friendship of Cunningham". Carlyle called him "a rugged, true mass of Scotch manhood" and the *Gallovidian Encyclopedia* describes him less turgidly as "cheerful in society, kind everywhere and liberal to the last degree . . . open and free, hides nothing, dashes on—a Scotchman every inch": a welcome change from the standard evocation of a "Scotchman". All the same, a few eyebrows must have been raised in amusement over the eulogy, for it was Cunningham's open boast that he could deceive "a whole General Assembly of Antiquarians", and he had actually and roundly deceived the Englishman, R. H. Cromek.

Cromek, a London engraver, laid himself temptingly open to deception. He appeared in Dumfries in 1809, avowedly to collect material for a new edition of Burns, but really hoping to join the famous collectors of Ballad fragments. "Gad, Sir!" said he to Cunningham, whose help he was trying to enlist, "if we could but make a volume! Gad Sir! see what Percy has done, and Ritson and Mr. Scott more recently with his *Border Ministrelsy*."

Unfortunately this appeal was made in the same breath with some criticism of Cunningham's own work, and criticism was not well received in that quarter. (Even a London editor's grammatical amendments to a contribution had been turned down: "Na, na; grammar or no grammar, it must go as I wrote it or not at all. We care nothing for the gender of pronouns in Nithsdale.") His revenge on the unwary Cromek was to assure him that Nithsdale abounded in ancient ballad fragments and then make them up himself.

He did it extremely well, and the result was triumphantly published in 1810 as *Remains of Galloway and Nithsdale Song*.

"Was it the duty of a son to show up the nakedness of his own land?" wrote the unrepentant Cunningham to a friend. "No. I went before to make the path straight. Keep it a secret!"

In spite of the deception, Cunningham's work had grown out of a genuine ear for the ballad tradition and a knowledge of Nithsdale lore. In the long-run it gained him a place among the minor poets of Scotland.

The material quoted here comes from the Appendix to the book, collected from old folk of Nithsdale well known to Cunningham and willing to trust him with their memories. It is said to be "truly descriptive" and beyond all suspicion of fraud, and there is no reason to doubt this.

Cunningham ended his career as secretary, adviser and friend to the sculptor Chantry, "beloved by his master".

THOMAS WILKIE

Wilkie was a medical student, born in Bowden and a collector of Border traditions in his spare time. Like Joseph Train he worked for Scott, though he had not Train's flair and was fatally inclined to "improve" the style of his material. But he was well aware that "as the aged drop into their graves, these spells and charms and ceremonies are buried along with them", and his MS. entitled "Old Rites, Ceremonies and Customs of the Inhabitants of the Southern Counties of Scotland" is something for which to be grateful.

ROBERT CHAMBERS AND CHARLES KIRKPATRICK SHARPE

Chambers' well-filled life took direction in good time with the discovery of the *Encyclopaedia Britannica* stowed away in an attic. To the ten-year-old this was worth more than a whole toyshop. He "roamed through it like a bee" and emerged all set not only for the publishing house of Chambers but for that rescue operation on Scotland's past out of which came the inimitable *Traditions of Edinburgh*, still a best seller.

Sixty-nine years—1802 to 1871—seem a short enough span for all Chambers set himself to accomplish and Scots who value their native tongue must be grateful that in the press of high enterprise he gave due and enlightened place to what he called "the simplicities of the uninstructed intellect". But for the *Popular Rhymes of Scotland*, "wherewith the cottage fireside was amused in days gone past", many of the Lowland tales would almost certainly have been lost, at least in their original language and form.

Chambers drew on every likely source for this book, but some of his best material came from a most unlikely one. Of all the inhabitants of Augustan Edinburgh, few could have seemed more remote from the cottage fireside than Charles Kirkpatrick Sharpe. Born in Hoddam Castle, graduate of Christ Church, intensely aristocratic, he was an artist, musician, wit, genealogical scandal-monger and merciless mocker of his fellow-men, sparing neither the "improving" zeal of the City Fathers (why not forward the sale of cabbages by boring a tunnel to the Grassmarket through the Castle rock, quell sectarian strife by transforming the High Kirk to the likeness of an ancient salt-cellar, and facilitate the recapture of hats blown off on the North Bridge by filling up the "uncouth valley" below?), nor the inhibitions of maiden ladies ("Every old maid when she hears of a marriage, purses up and prims her mouth as if she had a couple of sloes in it"). He could be kind, but everyone dreaded the rasp of his tongue except three people who had never felt it—his father and mother and Nurse Jenny, ruler of his childhood's nursery. She could even hold up the flow of epigrams in his student letters from Oxford—"How is Mammy Jenny?"—and long after her death he reproduced with loving accuracy the recitations which had drawn from her youthful audience admiring hugs and cries of terror and delight.

For richness of language and dramatic power, "Whuppity Stoorie", "Tibbie's Bairn" and "The Strange Visitor" are among the gems of Chambers' collection.

THE ETTRICK SHEPHERD

A definite setting can add conviction to the strangest experience. Even a touch of recognisable fact and the supernatural gains reality and dimension:

> As I was walking a' ma lane
> *Atween a water and a wa'.* . . .[1]

The ballad-makers had this secret of blending exactness with imagination but it was James Hogg who brought it in full measure to the enhancement of fairy literature. "He caught up", writes Professor Veitch, "several of the floating traditions which actually localised the fairy doings",[2] and as he herded his sheep in the utter solitude of those haunted places the legends became inseparable in his thought from the visible lie of the land, its scents and sounds, its flowers, birds, trees and weather—all most closely observed. The detailed accuracy of description brings to mind those small, authentic touches by which Gavin Douglas builds up his picture of a Lowland summer evening: "up gois the bat with her peelit lethryn flicht".[3] Hogg, in his younger days, had never so much as heard of the renaissance poets, but he was endowed with their capacity for strict observation.

His herding days began at the age of seven: a ewe lamb and a pair of shoes for a half year's wage. Schooling only lasted six months and he could barely pick out letters, let alone write them. An impossible starting point one would think for a literary career, and yet his highly individual genius had everything it needed—summer days by the Ettrick Water, the Douglas Burn, the Hawkshaw Rig, the Fairy Slack; winter nights in the cottage at Ettrickhall with his mother's vast store of Border lore poured out for his benefit. She claimed kinship with the notorious witch of Fauldshope,[4] and her fairy tales had all come down by word of mouth from ancient times.

> I learned them in the lonely glen
> The last abodes of living men,
> Where never stranger came our way
> By summer night, or winter day;
> Where neighbouring hind or cot was none . . .
> How stern and ample was the sway
> Of themes like these when darkness fell,
> When doors were barred and eldren dame
> Plied at her task beside the flame
> That through the smoke and gloom alone
> On dim and umber'd faces shone[5] . . .

His word picture is as evocative as a drawing by David Allan.

At sixteen, after nine years on the hills, Hogg assumed the shepherd's plaid with as much pride as Scott was to feel soon after on assuming the Advocate's gown. Service followed with the Laidlaws of Black House, bringing friendship and encouragement as well as the freedom of a considerable library. But even at twenty reading came slowly, while for the stern task of writing he found it necessary to strip to his shirt—only to be defeated after a few lines by a cramped wrist.

Nevertheless, the poems were written and printed. He met Scott and the kindred spirits of the Abbotsford circle. His sturdy figure was seen more often in Edinburgh and at last, in 1813, *The Queen's Wake* roused the literary world: "when," it wondered, "shall we see such another shepherd?"—a question to be repeated even more cogently with the appearance of the *Justified Sinner*. But it is with the Notes to *The Queen's Wake* that this collection is concerned.

NOTES

1. I am indebted for this example to Miss Rhoda Spence.
2. John Veitch, *History and Poetry of the Scottish Border*.
3. Introduction to the *Aeneid*.
4. See the tale "Witch and Warlock".
5. James Hogg, *Poetical Works*.

WILLIAM NICHOLSON

One fine spring morning of the early nineteenth century a Kirkcudbright man, riding past St. Mary's Isle, was startled by the sound of music. Leaving his horse, he crossed a field and found a packman tuning his pipes in a quarry hole for the benefit of half a dozen wild young colts, who leapt and capered with delight, throwing up their heels and pausing now and then to snort their applause. "And I have mair pleesure", announced the packman, "in piping to thae daft cowts than if the best ladies in a' the land had been figuring away to my poor music."

In this engaging scene we have a glimpse of William Nicholson, author of "The Brownie of Blednoch", and a most characteristic one, for, with all his shortcomings, he had "a gladness of heart as when one goeth forth with a pipe".

Like Hogg, Nicholson was born in poverty. An "auld clay biggin" at Tannymaas in the Galloway parish of Borgue was his home and—again like Hogg—his best education came from his mother's store of legends, traditions and "whole blads of poetry", which she dispensed as she drew out her thread under a hawthorn bush on summer afternoons—she had known a man whose mother had to face the Kirk Session over his abduction by the fairies. At school the boy was almost impervious to instruction, but left to himself he devoured anything in print that came his way, carrying the spoil to the lee of a dyke or planting where even in winter he would crouch for hours, oblivious of cold.

When he was fourteen they equipped him with a wooden box and fifteen shillings worth of pins, needles, thimbles, scissors and small-wares and sent him off, with his pipes, to tramp the countryside. His make-up being "fifty parts poetry, forty of music and only ten of business ability", this fell short of a success story, though he did build up a reputation for muslins and ribbons. But a packman's life provided plenty of time for verse-making and after twenty-five years of it he had enough poetry in hand to "see what printing a book would do". The book appeared in 1814, bringing £100 to replenish his pack, and a good measure of appreciation. Hogg and Cunningham both thought highly of his work, the Duke of Buccleuch was one of his patrons, and the prospects seemed bright; but in spite of much encouragement there were only flashes of that "indescribable, inestimable, unmistakable impress of genius" which Dr. John Brown discerned in "The Brownie". He died, poverty-stricken, in 1814. But he was rich in friends and his songs are still sung in Galloway.

Some Forgotten Occupations

THE HERB WIFE

"For the cure of children that were backgaen (usually through having got the waff o' an ill e'e) there was a specific, the recipe for which was handed down the generations in a few families—a decoction of herbs gathered at certain periods of the moon. An Herb Wife with this secret was important in the community. She was sent for from a great distance, taken ben the house, and never allowed to leave without a plentiful bountith of mutton, ham, butter and scon-meal.

"Magsie Moran was an Herb Wife: she wonned amang the moors at the head of Ken Water. Her garb, when on herb-gathering excursions, was a green and black chequered plaid wrapped round her body and fastened with a pin made of a sheep's shank-bane, her head partially covered with a folded red and blue handkerchief from under which, before and behind, hung grizzled elf-locks like the main of a muirland gallowa'; she never went abroad without a goodly kent like a packman's pike-staff. Her song ran thus:

> Polypodie on the oak
> Polypodie on the rock
> Polypodie on the oak's
>   the best polypodie.
> Elf shot girse and maiden hair
> Pu' them ere the birk's bare,
> Flatterbaw ye mauna spare
> To mingle in yere crowdie."

> *The Castle Douglas Miscellany*

THE COWAR-WOMAN

There was also the Cowar-woman, a maker of broom couws or besoms. "A wisp of broom, also called a cow or couw, is sometimes used for a temporary blaze on poor hearths in Scotland."

The Carlyles, driving from Borland to Craigenputtock, saw her in a winter landscape: . . . "heart of winter, intense calm frost . . . past the base of towering New Abbey, huge ruins, piercing grandly into the silent frosty sunset . . . and the poor old Cowar-woman offering to warm us with a flame of dry broom, 'A'll licht a bruim couw, if ye'll please to come in'."

> Thomas Carlyle, *Reminiscences*

THE WANDERING FIDDLER

"I had visited a friend at the Ferrytown of Cree and was returning to Newton Stewart when I met on the way the Blind Musician with his harp over his shoulder led by his wife and followed by some children walking and others in a small wicker cart drawn by a little cuddie of the old gypsy kind. As I drew near the old man raised his harp and began to play the popular air "Kenmure's Up and Awa', Willie".

"It was a calm evening in the month of April and the sound of the harp soon brought a crowd of peasants from the neighbouring fields of Kirroughtrees and the hamlet of Machermore which, with a fiddle played by one of the younger branches of the Minstrel's family, formed a band that called into action the dancing powers not only of the other children but several of the spectators.

"The Blind Minstrel was upwards of fifty years of age and of very diminutive stature. The small part of his countenance to be seen above his bushy beard was of a sallow complexion, very much pitted by smallpox, and was nowise improved by his sightless eyeballs which rolled as he moved his hand along the harp strings. His habiliments seemed to be just what chance had thrown in his way. On his legs he wore a pair of blue rigg-and-fur (ribbed) hoeskins partly drawn over the knees of his small clothes. His vest of red plush cloth with deep pockets hanging over the thighs was in every way similar to that kept in the wardrobe of Eglinton Castle stained with the blood of the unfortunate Earl who was shot by Campbell the exciseman. The outside colour of his coat was brown, the inside blue. On his head he wore the cap called in old times a Megiskie, with a large Roman letter in front, such as was usually worn by Chattering Charlie the last professional jester in the family of Cassilis.

"His wife wore on her head an old Bandanna handkerchief loosely tied below her chin with one corner hanging between her shoulders over the hood of a dark duffled Cardinal, the tail of which was long.

"The old man and his wife seemed themselves to enjoy the felicity which their music imparted to others. They thankfully received the small sum collected for them, and moved away in search of a resting place for the night."

On that evening they found lodgings at Skyreburn, but two nights later were forced to camp in a gravel pit near Twynholm. The brow of the pit collapsed, killing the whole family in their sleep. They might not even have been found but for the distress of their ass which paced up and down all next day, braying on its master. The family were buried in Twynholm kirkyard at the expense of the Kirk Session.

This blind fiddler, William ap Pritchard, was a native of Carnarvonshire, but had lived long in the South of Scotland. "At merrymakings in Town and at Kirns in the country he was the chief 'gutscraper' between Gretna Green and the Braes of Glenapp, and was noted for giving the longest Reel for a penny of any fiddler."

> Letter from Joseph Train to Scott, 1816. (This fiddler was the prototype of the Blind Fiddler in *Redgauntlet*.)

Working Stones in the Days of the Tales

In the high days of the Tales, when Angus men still stooked their corn on stachles and Edinburgh schoolboys played the game of chuckies, life in Scotland was dominated by stones. Not the brooding Dark Age monuments, but the friendly necessities of house, steading and field. The knocking-stones, bannock-stones, querns, skew-stones, loom-stones, tippet-stones,[1] brig-stones, kep-stones, thruch-stones[2] and many others once in common use are now as thoroughly forgotten as the masons, dykers and road-menders who handled them with knowledge and respect. Their very names are slipping away. Plastic has put a ruthless end to the immemorial age of stone.

Between them, the knocking-stone and the quern span history from palaeolithic times to the beginning of the twentieth century. The saddle quern was hoary with age when Samson "did grind in the prison house", but the rotary type was new when the two women went grinding together in the New Testament. That same type was used by the women of Scotland until the seventeenth century, when the revenue possibilities of the verticle mill became obvious to the Government and a law of 1641 decreed that all "quarnis" were to be broken. ". . . ilk tenant and cottar to goe with their grindable cornes to the milnes whereto they are thirled, under pain of ten pounds." But the knocking of barley for broth was still allowed—the old reel "Kail and Knockit Corn" is a memory of the farm hands' regulation supper—while the Islands remained faithful for another two or three centuries to their grinding stones and the ancient songs that belonged to them: in some remote parts these stones were so much valued that they were ceremonially rubbed with a wisp of straw every Saturday night.

The round stone on which bannocks were baked and its little brother that toasted them come up also from the depths of time, encrusted with old beliefs. These kindly stones, once found on every hearth, are rarely seen nowadays even in museums. One was ploughed up recently on an Angus farm, almost undamaged, a round block of red sandstone about eleven inches in diameter. Part of a marriage plenishing, it bears the date 1707, along with initials and a true lovers' knot, thus linking the daily bread of the family to the inner meaning of home. Small wonder that these bannock-stones were handed down the generations. Even the fairies used them, if we are to believe a certain old man "too wise to walk into a well" who assured Mrs. Grant of Laggan that he had often relished the smell of the good folks' bannocks toasting as he passed their hillocks on Corrieyairack, early in the morning and "far from human dwellings".

The pun'-stane and the meal-stane quarter once lay handy in the farm-house kitchens of Galloway. These were sea-stones, gathered from the shore, roughly adjusted to official weights but erring on the generous side in their measures of butter and meal.

Once it was considered a wise precaution to cast three stones into the sea before bathing. Just before her execution Mary, Queen of Scots sent her brother-in-law of France "two rare stones valuable for health" along with touching wishes for a long and happy life. A stone amulet set in silver and worn by Sir Walter Scott's mother is kept at Abbotsford; and Haddington can show a grave-stone, just too narrow for its pious epitaph which was accordingly stripped of its final letter—and its piety. It reads, "O Lord she was Thin". Such things have a preserving touch of the fantastic and will no doubt survive. But with the honest old working stones it is another matter. The troughs and bowls of every shape and size, once so essential in kitchen and steading; the stones placed on village greens for the communal beating of flax; the slabs on which apprentice masons practised their letters; the cat-stanes[3] against which cottage fires were built; the weight-stones, tether-stones, mounting-stones, mill-stones and lintels; the collady-stones decking window-sills and garden paths; even the humble stukie—they are all disappearing, despised or merely unrecognised.[4]

"Living plastic" would be an absurd if not downright blasphemous combination of words; but to talk of living stone is the acknowledgement of an ancient significance. And how the mediaeval colours—the perse, cinnabar, crammasie, lattour, sorrel and damask of the poets—must have gleamed against its grey background!

NOTES

1. Tippet-stone, a round stone with a hook for twisting rope or hair.
2. A thruch-stane is a flat gravestone (derived from the Anglo-Saxon *thrugh*—a sarcophagus) and should be distinguished from a through-stane, which went right through the thickness of a wall.
3. The cat-stane or cat-herd or cheek-stane supported the old grates, one on either side: derivation quite simple—the cat liked to sit on them.
4. A fine collection of domestic stones can be seen in the garden of Broughton House, Kirkcudbright.

Bread in the Days of the Tales

Bread, usually in the form of a bannock, has a special place in the context of the Tales. Recognised as the end product of that arduous cycle of ploughing, sowing, reaping, threshing and grinding, which held small communities together and literally kept them in life, it had both a religious and an economic significance. The invisible and the visible were focussed together in that small round object toasting on the bannock stone, and in some parts of the West Highlands it actually symbolised the Eucharist. Even in the post-Reformation Lowlands, to waste bread or treat it carelessly was considered not only blame-worthy but profane.

Certain superstitions belonged to the baking of bannocks— they had to be kneaded sunwise (the Druids had cast a long shadow); a broken crown meant the approach of a stranger, and the disposal of left-over meal was fraught with dangers. But behind the "freits" there was always a genuine sense of reverence for the staff of life.

The term "bannock" is a wide one. Mactaggart's *Gallovidian Encyclopedia* describes it as a round, thin cake, often with a hole in the centre and says that "if haurned or toasted on the burning seeds of the shelled oats it is as brittle as if baked with butter". Millbannocks, a foot in diameter, were often baked thus in the mill itself. Ingredients varied with the national economy— bannocks have always been tied to the standard of living. Grey oats, grown in the early centuries, produced the quickly made Graddan bannock—from field to table in one hour: a speed achieved by burning the grain from the ear, grinding it on the ever-ready quern and baking it forthwith on a hot stone. An Act of 1457, causing every husbandman who tilled with the plough and seven oxen to sow yearly a firlot of peas and forty beans, brought in the Mashlum bannock, mixed with barley and pulses. Also, according to the current crop, there were pease bannocks, barley bannocks, bere bannocks and hauvermeal bannocks. Family occasions added variety—the crying bannock for a birth, followed in due course by the teething bannock; while special bannocks marked the quarters of the year.

Other forms of bread did exist, but sparsely. Wheat was reserved for such high purposes as the payment of clergy stipends, so it was late in the eighteenth century before the wheaten loaf began to appear for general use. Flourocks, or scones made with flour, were so rare a delicacy that when a certain Border housewife died the spontaneous cry was: "She's ta'en guid care to eat a' the flourocks afore she crossed the Jordan!" But the faithful bannock was the mainstay.

Respect for bread was, of course, strengthened by its scarcity. Poverty and famine with all their wretchedness were so familiar and so deeply ground into the national consciousness that even the children's rhymes echoed them:

> . . . let the weary herdies in,
> A' weetie, a' weary,
> A' drookit, a' dreary;
> I haena gotten a bite the day but a sup o' cauld sowens . . .

As an evocation of those recurring "lean years" when the price of grain soared and labourers, tightening their belts at noon, drank from the burn instead of eating, this is more direct than any official record.

Carlyle has described the plight of his grandmother in the seventeen-sixties, exposed to great privations and reduced at times, in spite of gallant efforts, to an empty girnel. On one of these occasions a bag of meal, long overdue, arrived late at night when the almost starving household was in bed. She rose to receive it, tore straw from her mattress—the only fuel she had—set bannocks to bake and roused the children for necessary food. A poignant moment in the long history of the bannock.

The Language of the Tales

The language of the Tales (with a few obvious exceptions) is the simple, spoken Scots of the eighteenth and nineteenth centuries. Since the narrators come from different parts of Scotland no attempt has been made to standardise spelling, vocabulary, syntax and usage. Many of the narrators (as distinct from the collectors) were probably illiterate.

The language of Lowland Scotland has been variously known as Scots, Broad Scots and the Doric. The first of these terms is preferred, the second acceptable and the third unhelpful, since Doric is simply the Greek term for a provincial dialect. It should be noted that the language of the Tales is not Lallans, which is an attempt by modern Scottish poets to re-create the literary mediaeval Scots of the makars.

Scots (to use the correct term) finds its highest written expression in the poetry of Ferguson and Burns, but it has very few monuments in prose. True, the novels of Scott, Galt and Stevenson abound in passages of richest vernacular Scots, but these are mainly pieces of dialogue—another illustration that Scots is essentially a spoken language and not a written one. Scott and Stevenson each wrote one masterpiece entirely in Scots—the short stories *Wandering Willie's Tale* and *Thrawn Janet*—but neither author could have sustained a full-length novel in that medium. Indeed, these two stories are in the nature of dramatic monologues.

Extravagant claims have been made on behalf of the Scots language. Lord Jeffrey said that it was "not to be considered as a provincial dialect . . . it is the language of the whole country . . . the common speech of the whole nation in early life and of many of its most exalted and accomplished individuals throughout their whole existence"; and Ruskin called it "the richest, subtlest, most musical of the living dialects of Europe". In view of these claims, and many others like them, it is important to note exactly what Scots was. In origin it was the speech of the Anglian settlers of the province of Northumbria, which extended from York to Edinburgh. It is, therefore, fundamentally an English dialect; and Sir William Wallace, the Scottish Patriot, spoke what his contemporaries were at pains to describe as "Ingils", although no doubt the tongue had by this time developed characteristics which distinguished it from the main Northumbrian dialect.

Later in the Middle Ages, the Scots speech spread north to the Highland line, over the north-eastern coastal plain, and into Orkney and Shetland, and this is as far as it ever went. Northwest of the Highland line, Gaelic was spoken; and when Gaelic declined it was replaced by a speech more akin to standard English than to Lowland Scots. Hence the once popular notion that the purest form of spoken English was to be heard in the streets of Inverness and hence the fact that few natives of the Highlands are to this day able to appreciate or understand the poetry of Burns.

However picturesque it may be, therefore, the Scots language has a very ordinary pedigree, similar to that of the Lancashire dialect. The supposed (and sometimes real) similarities between Scots and German are only what one would expect to find in two Germanic languages: the same similarities would be found in many another English dialect. The difference between Scots and Gaelic is complete, and there are remarkably few loan-words from one to the other.

The language of the Tales, then, is that of the restricted area of Lowland Scotland, and indeed this is the extent of the world which they describe. It is a less well-known world than the Highland one of kilts and claymores, heather and mountains, and its language is rapidly passing out of use. In both these senses it is our forgotten heritage.

GLOSSARY AND NOTES ON WORDS

IT was Margaret Laidlaw who voiced the instinctive reluctance of the story-teller to have the living, tuneable word locked up in print. "Oo, na, na, sir," runs her well-known complaint to Scott, "it was never prentit i' the warld. Ma brithers an' me learned it frae auld Andrew Moor, an' he learned it an' mony mae frae auld Babby Mettlin, that was housckeeper to the first Laird o' Tushilaw . . . and ye hae spoilt them a'thegether . . . they're nouther richt spell'd, nor richt setten doon."

Margaret Laidlaw would have objected even more strongly to the notes which follow; she would no doubt have held that the only way to explain to somebody what *spurtle* or *coggie* means is to show him the implement itself. Nevertheless, the editor has decided with some trepidation to offer explanation of certain words which may be unfamiliar to the southern reader or which are interesting in themselves. Words which differ only slightly from their "richt spell'd" English equivalents (e.g. *ain* for own) have not been included.

Abune, above.
Airn, iron.
Airt, airth, direction, quarter.
Aisins, easins, eaves; the space between the wall-head and the rafters, known also as *the crap o' the wa'*.
Ajee, aside, awry; also ajar.
Amaist, almost.
An, if.
Ase, asse, alse, ashes.
Aucht, (i) to own (double meaning of possess and owe); (ii) aught, anything.
Ava', at all (lit. of all) (cf. French *pas du tout*).

Backend, autumn.
Back-gaen, not thriving.
Baudrons, a cat; *baud* originally meant a hare; and cf. French *ronron*, purr.
Bawbee, a halfpenny.
Beel, beal, to suppurate, fester (cognate with boil).
Begood, began.
Begunk, to cheat, deceive, beguile.
Bicker, (i) a wooden drinking bowl, in well-to-do houses often tipped with silver (cf. beaker); (ii) to move quickly, noisily; to quarrel.

Bigg, to build; *biggin*, a building.

Bield, a shelter; but in *The Herd's Tale* it means "bold".

Birse, bristle, hair; (fig.) anger.

Blad, a sheet or leaf (cf. German *Blatt*).

Blinman's baws, puff balls.

Bluidy fingers, foxgloves.

Bourtree, an elder. (Bower tree, from its habitual shape.)

Bowte, a bolt; *to play bowte*, to rebound, as when a bolt is shot.

Brae, hill, slope; *braeheid*, hilltop.

Brat, an apron, cloth.

Braws, finery, beautiful things; *braw*, fine (lit. brave).

Breek, to tuck up. Women *breeked* their petticoats for shearing in wet weather; *Are ye gaun to breek the day?*

Brose, unboiled porridge made by pouring boiling water on meal; *kale brose*, shredded kail boiled with oatmeal in stock (as applied to the unfortunate Cuddie Headrig by Jennie Dennison); *yowe brose*, brose made with ewe's milk.

Bucht, a sheepfold; to herd sheep; *bucht-fluke*, sheepfold gate (see under *Flake*).

Bud, *bude*, behoved (contracted first to *behude*, then *bude*).

Buddo, term of endearment addressed to a child (Orkney and Shetland).

Busk, to prepare, make ready, dress.

But and ben, the *but* was the outer (kitchen) room, *ben* the inner (best) room, together making the traditional two-roomed dwelling, *but and ben*. Derives from Old English *be-utan*—without and *be-innan*—within. Thus the phrase in the *Red Etin* rhyme means "sniff throughout the house". The Wee Bunnock runs *ben the hoose* (entry) and *but the hoose* (exit).

Callant, a lad (usually affectionate).

Cannie, careful, cautious; *cannie wife*, midwife.

Cantie, comfortable, cheerful, lively.

Cap, *cappy*, *caup*, a wooden bowl for food or drink; *he's as fu' as cap or stoup'll mak' him.*

Carlin, an old woman, witch (fem. of *carle*).

Cazy, *cassie*, a straw creel.

Chafer, a chafing dish, also blacksmith's implement.

Chap, a tap or knocking.

Champit, mashed.

Chessel, a cheese vat.

Chiel, a fellow, a child, a servant.

Clash, gossip, scandal; *carried clash*—hearsay. Also a large quantity of anything; a cow might give *a clash of milk*.

Cleekit, caught or hooked up. Also *cleek*, to cheat; *He'll cleek ye, gin he can.*

Cleugh, a gorge, chasm, or the rocks surrounding it.

Clout, (i) to patch or mend (usually clothes); (ii) to beat; (iii) a cloth.

Close, a passage, lane.

Clove, to break the fibre of flax before heckling; the instrument for doing this.

Clue, thread.

Cog, coggie, a small wooden pail or bowl for milk or broth.

Contramawcious, perverse, self-willed. (Corruption of contumacious with idea of *contra* added.)

Cottar, a cottager; *cottar-house,* a tied house for a farm servant.

Coup, to overturn, tip, fall.

Couples, cupples, sloping rafters.

Cow, Cowe, (i) a turf; (ii) a branch; slip of wood.

Craig, a rock, crag.

Cribbie, a measure in weaving: "as much yarn as goes half-way round the reel".

Cringlo, a footstool.

Croon, "the melancholy music of the Ox". (Mactaggart.)

Crowdie, (i) oatmeal mixed with cold water; (ii) a kind of soft cheese.

Cubby, a basket made of heather or straw, slung on the back.

Cuddie, a small horse.

Cuff, the nape of the neck.

Cuist, to cast, throw.

Curchie, a curtsey.

Cuttie, cutty, short, small, diminutive; thus, a young woman. See also *Sark.*

Daffin', jaunty behaviour, often in the sense of folly; *play is good but daffin' dow not.*

Darg, a day's work, a task (reduced form of Old English *daegweorc* meaning day's work).

Dern, secret, hidden.

Dicht, to wipe clean, rub, sweep; to give someone a buffet or a dressing down.

Ding, to knock or beat; defeat or overcome.

Dirl, to cause to vibrate; a painful blow.

Disjaskit, in disrepair, depressed, weary.

Donnert, scatterbrained; (from *daundered* meaning wandered).

Doo, a pigeon, dove.

Douce, sober, modest.

Doup, the buttocks. That part of the human anatomy which Sir Walter Scott called "the sitting end", but freely used for the lower end of almost anything; *the doup o' the day,* evening; *the doup o' e'en,* late evening; *the day's doupin' doon,* it's getting late.

Dowie, sad, weary, dispirited.

Dree, (i) to suspect, fear (short for dread); (ii) to suffer, endure: *dree your weird,* suffer your fate.

Drooth, a drought, thirst.

Drumlie, cloudy, muddy, gloomy, sullen.

Dwammy, faint.

Dwyne, to dwindle, waste away, fade. Also *dwimmil*: *the aits a' dwimmilt awa' afore they ripened,* the oats wasted before they were ripe.

Dulefu', sorrowful, in the sense of causing pain.

Een, the eyes; *ill-een*, evil eyes.

Enoo, now, just now, soon (lit. even now).

Ether-stane, an adder stone. A small perforated stone or bead used as an amulet.

Ettle, intend, plan, aim.

Fail, turf used for building dykes, etc.

Farrand, seeming; *fair farrand*, good-looking (opposite of *foul-farrand*); *auld farrand*, old fashioned.

Fash, to trouble (cf. French, *fâcher*, to annoy).

Fauld, a pen, fold; *fauld-dyke*, the wall of a sheep pen.

Feat, neatly made (perhaps from French, *fait*).

Fell, very (degree).

Fendin', a provision; *left wi' sma' fendin'*, ill-provided for.

Ferlie, (i) a strange phenomenon, marvel; (ii) a fairy.

Fient, emphatic negative; *the fient a body*, not a person, nobody; *fient hait*, not a whit. Derived from *fiend* and "used perhaps by some who are not aware that it is in fact an invocation of the devil".

Firsle, to rustle.

Fit, foot.

Flake, fluke, a fence, hurdle, gate, rack, lattice.

Flatterbaw, butterburr.

Fleg, fley, to frighten. "It would seem that fly and fley in all their senses originally denoted the flight of birds."

Fleech, fleitch, to flatter, cajole.

Flit, to remove, shift to fresh grazing, move to a new house.

Flyte, to quarrel, scold.

Forbye, (i) besides; (ii) except.

Forfochten, exhausted, worn out (lit. fought out).

Four-oorie, a four-hourly feed.

Freit, superstitious belief or act.

Fremyt, strange; *fremyt folk*, strangers (cf. German, *fremd*).

Fuss, to fetch.

Gab, the mouth; *to gab*, to speak; *the gift of the gab*, fluency in speech.

Gabbit, concerning the mouth; *shuttle-gabbit*, an untranslatable description of a person with a protruding jaw. In Roxburghshire, *gowan-gabbit*, applied to a very bright morning, is a prediction of rain.

Gar, to cause, make.

Gate, gait, gaet, a way, road, street; *onygate*, anyway.

Gaudsman, the man who prodded the plough-horses or oxen with his *gaud* or iron bar.

Gaunt, gant, to yawn.

Gerse, girse, grass. (Metathesis (transposition of letters) is common in dialect words, e.g. below becomes *ablow*, bristle, *birsle* (q.v.); board, *brod* (*dambrod*, a chequerboard); scratch, *scart*.)

Get, contemptuous word for a child, from the verb beget. Can also be used affectionately: *the getlins*, the little ones.

Gilpin, a frolicksome youngster (cf. French *galopin*, errand boy). Also used for swirling water; *gilp*, a splash; *to gilp*, to jerk.

Gin, if.

Gled, a kite. Gives the place name Gledstanes (*anglice*, Gladstone).

Gliff, (i) a sudden fright or shock; (ii) glimpse, glance.

Glower, to scowl, stare intently.

Goose, a tailor's iron, so-called because the handle was shaped like a goose's neck.

Gowan, a daisy.

Gowk, a cuckoo. Also a simpleton. Why the word for cuckoo, that most astute of birds, should also be used for a fool is obscure although it has been suggested that both bird and man tend to harp too long on one subject.

Gowpen, a handful (usually double, two hands together as a scoop); *a gowpenfu' o' stour mak's a nievefu' o' glaur*, two handfuls of dust make a fistful of mud.

Greet, to weep; *grat*, wept; *begrutten*, tearstained.

Grieshoch, the burning embers, especially of peat (cf. *grushach*, Dumfriesshire; *griosach*, Gaelic).

Gropus, *gropius*, *carle-Gropus*, a stupid person.

Gryse, a pig or piglet; *stickit gryse*, a stuck pig.

Hafflins, partly, nearly; *a hafflin'*, a youngster (half-grown).

Hail, to pour; *hailin' on*, raining heavily.

Hait, a very small quantity, a whit.

Halve-net, a bag-shaped net set to catch fish as the tide ebbs.

Hantle, a considerable quantity.

Happock, a little hump. To *hap* means to wrap or cover, and a *happock* is a piece of covered ground, usually a knoll. The diminutive ending is characteristic (cf. *knappock* (little knob), *winnock* (window), *hillock*, etc.).

Haud, to hold.

Haurn, to toast.

Haver, *haiver*, to talk nonsense; *haivers*, nonsense.

Havermeal, *hauvermeal*, oatmeal; *haverpoke*, a horse's nosebag (cf. haversack).

Heckle, a toothed implement for dressing flax. The heckler's job was to separate tow from lint, and whether this class of person was politically motivated or whether the job itself had some figurative significance, a heckler came to mean a vociferous critic. A *heckle-pin* was the tooth of a steel comb; the *Muir o' Heckle-pins* was a children's game. (See *Dialect of Bunffshire*, Gregor, 1866.) To be kept on heckle-pins was to be in a state of suspense, and in Angus heckle biscuits had pin-holes in them.

Hempy, a rogue, often used indulgently. Originally a gallows bird, destined for a hempen rope.

Herry, to rob or plunder (same as harry).

Hind, a servant.

Hizzie, a hussy (corruption of housewife).

Holm, flat ground beside a river.

Houlet, howlet, hoolet, an owl.
Howd, to swing, bob up and down.
Howe, a hollow, lowest part; *how o' the nicht,* midnight.
Howk, dig, unearth (containing the idea of "to hollow").
Hugger, an old stocking used as a purse; a hoard. (See notes, p. 23.)
Hum, bad humour or bad odour.
Hurcheon, a hedgehog.

Ilk, ilka, (i) each, every; (ii) the same; *of that ilk,* of the same. Thus, Moncreiffe (the family) of Moncreiffe (the place) is *Moncreiffe of that Ilk;* very often misused to mean "of that sort" or "like that".
Ingle, a fire burning on a hearth.

Jad, jaud, a perverse woman (originally a mare); cf. English, jade.
Jaw, to pour, spill; *jawbox,* water trough; *jaw-hole,* a primitive drain.
Jink, a quick, sudden movement; *play jink aboot,* to dodge.
Jokus, jovial, given to joking.

Kail, cabbage, more esp. borecole; *kailyard,* cabbage patch, kitchen garden.
Kaim, kame, a comb.
Keek, to peep, glance.
Kemp, to strive or compete (cf. German *kämpfen,* to struggle; *Mein Kampf,* my struggle).
Kent, a long shepherd's staff, used e.g. for vaulting ditches.
Kep, to catch.
Kerl, a tall candlestick.
Kimmer, cummer, a gossip, witch (cf. French *commère,* godmother).
Kintra, country.
Kirn, churn.
Kist, a chest, trunk; *kist o' whistles,* an organ.
Kitchen, relish. A host would studiously avoid placing guests of the same sex next to each other at table on the principle that *butter to butter is nae kitchen*—a savoury sandwich must have meat in the middle; *kitchenless,* savourless.
Knapock, knablock, a knob.
Knoit, to knock, esp. of the knees.
Kye, cattle.
Knowe, a hillock, mound, often associated with fairies (cognate with knoll).

Lade, an artificial watercourse, a millrace (containing the idea of water being "led").
Lair, a place for lying down. A version of the 23rd Psalm runs:
　　　　"He makes my lair / In fields most fair . . ."
Also used for material spread out to dry, e.g. a peat-lair.
Lappert, curdled, as milk in thundery weather; *lappered milk kebbocks,* sour milk cheese.
Langsyne, long since. Probably not one Scot in ten, nor one Englishman in a

hundred, knows that *Auld Lang Syne* means The Days that are No
More.

Lave, that which is left over, the remainder, the rest (literally, the leave).

Lawbrod, the tailor's ironing board.

Lease, to release. *Early that leases me*, "in that case I shall soon be free".

Leugh, to laugh, laughed.

Leuk, to see to something.

Lick, to smack, wallop.

Limmer, a rogue, a troublesome woman.

Lingle, a cobbler's waxed thread; same derivation as linen.

Linn, a waterfall, gorge, deep pool.

Lintie, a linnet.

Lippen, to trust.

Lish, *lith*, nimble.

Loof, *luif*, *lufe*, the palm of the hand. An old form of flat curling stone was
called a *loofy*.

Loon, a lad.

Loup, *lowp*, to leap; *loup the hool*, to slip the moorings.

Louthe, abundance; more commonly *routh*.

Lowne, *loune*, calm; *it's growing lowne*, the wind's falling.

Luckie, *lucky*, an old woman; *luckie-minnie*, grandmother; occasionally,
luckie-daddie.

Lug, an ear.

Lum, a chimney.

Mart, *mert*, provision, especially for winter (contracted form of market).

Maun, must; *mauna*, must not.

Mell, a mallet, heavy hammer (cf. Latin *malleus*).

Mickle, *muckle*, large, big; much (see *puckle*).

Minnie, *minny*, mother.

Mirk, darkness.

Mool, *moul*, crumbled earth. In plural, associated with the kirkyard.

Moolins, crumbs.

Moudiewart, a mole (lit. "earth-thrower"). Also used of a small, dark, hairy
person.

Mutch, a cap of white linen or muslin worn by a married woman; also a
baby's bonnet (cf. German *Mütze*).

Napple root, "a sweet, wild root; heath peas. The black knotty root of a herb
diligently digged for and greedily chewed by boys; its taste being rather
pleasant." Mactaggart, *Gallovidian Encyclopedia*.

Neb, a nose, beak.

Neist, next.

Nieve, a hand, fist; *thy nieve's here*, your hand is in this.

Nor, than.

Onstead, a cluster of farm cottages.

Oorie, uncanny, gloomy. (Associated but not cognate with eerie.)

Or, (i) before; (ii) until. (This word is the same as "ere", with the important difference that it is not so pronounced; and "or" is a poor phonetic rendering, for the sound of the word is practically vowel-less. The word is still widely used in Scotland, and the threat *Wait 'r yer faither comes hame* has not yet lost all its effectiveness.)

Paddo, paddock, a frog.

Park, an enclosed pasture, a field. (*Field* itself in Scots meant unenclosed cultivated land, and was therefore not the same as park. Neither term denotes a pleasure-ground.)

Pech, a deep breath; to pant.

Peerie, small, little, tiny (current only in Orkney and Shetland). *Peerie folk,* fairies.

Pew, an expression of disapproval.

Philabeg, a kilt (properly, little kilt, i.e. that part worn round the waist and separate from the plaid.)

Pig, an earthen vessel; a *hinnie-pig* holds honey. A *piggerie* was a pottery and the *pig-man* sold crockery from door to door.

Pirn, a spool for taking yarn; a reel. *Pirnit,* interwoven. A *pirnie-cap* was a night-cap striped in red, white and blue. The pastor of Stobo in the mid-sixteenth century had gloves *pirnit with gold. He's wun himsel' intil a fine pirn,* he's got himself into a difficulty.

Platt, to plait, pleat.

Plough-sock, a ploughshare.

Pooch, a pocket, pouch.

Pook, pouk, to pluck.

Poother, powder.

Pow, (i) a pool, creek, quay; (ii) a head.

Pownie, a pony.

Precentor, the singer who leads the church congregation in praise.

Preen, a pin.

Premeese, to suppose.

Press, a cupboard.

Prie, pree, to taste, sample (short for *preeve,* cf. French *éprouver*).

Prig, to haggle, beseech (cf. Latin *precare* to pray).

Puckle, pickle, a small quantity or particle of any kind (lit. a grain). (*Muckle/mickle* signifies a large quantity. It is therefore nonsense to say *Mony a mickle makes a muckle*: the correct version of the proverb is *Mony a puckle maks a muckle.*)

Pyke, pike, to pick; *pykit,* meagre-looking.

Pyock, a bag, poke.

Rade, a riding, a mounted foray.

Randy, aggressive, irrepressible.

Rashes, reeds or rushes; *rashiecoat,* a coat of rushes.

Rax, to reach out, stretch, strain; *rax me the Buik* was often the preliminary to family worship.

Ream, cream, froth (cf. German, *Rahm*).

Reck, to matter; *what recks?* what does it matter?

Redd, to put in order, clear out; as an adj., active—*a redd servant.*

Rede, red. As used in *Aiken Drum* it is probably short for *rede-wud*, mad.

Reek, smoke (cf. German *Rauch*); *Auld Reekie* was the name given to Edinburgh before most of it became a smokeless zone.

Riddle, a coarse-meshed sieve. (Riddles were used for divination as well as for ridding oneself of a fairy changeling, not to mention more mundane purposes.)

Riggin, the ridge of a roof.

Ripe, *rype*, to search. Also *ripe the ribs*, poke the fire; *rype-pouch*, pickpocket.

Rive, *ryve*, a split; to burst, tear. In the old days of frugality it was *better the belly rive nor guid meat connacht*—eat till you burst rather than waste good food.

Rivlin, a shoe made out of undressed hide; also *rullion.*

Rock, a distaff, spindle.

Roose, to rouse (of a fire, blaze up).

Routh, abundance. Cf. Roxburghshire phrase *Gie him routh and scouth*—give (a child) good food and freedom.

Rug, to pull, tug.

Rump, to plunder, clean out of money.

Sain, to protect by a ritual act, e.g. make a sign of the cross; to bless.

Sair, sore.

Sark, a man's shirt or a woman's chemise. *Cutty Sark* was Tam o' Shanter's enthusiastic term for the dancing girl in the short shift.

Saugh, *saugh-tree*, a willow. Cognate with English *sallow* and Irish *sally.*

Sauster, a pudding made from minced meat and meal, sliced and fried (cf. French, *saucisse*).

Scaith, harm.

Scale, *skail*, to spill or scatter; used of people as well as of commodities— *the kirk scailed*, the congregation dispersed.

Scart, to scratch, scrape.

Scaud, (i) to scald, wither, pain, vex; (ii) a glimpse, tinge.

Scaudman's heid, a sea urchin.

Scraich, *skraich*, to scream, shriek.

Scrieve, to move, glide, speed on; as a noun, something written.

Scunner, abhorrence; as a verb, to flinch or recoil.

Seely, happy in the sense of blessed (cf. German *seelig*, denoting inner joy).

Segg, the yellow flag iris.

Selk, *selch*, a seal; *selkie folk*, a fabulous race of creatures, half-seal half-human, in the mythology of Orkney and Shetland.

Shears, scissors.

Shiel, a shelter (cf. shieling, Galashiels).

Sicker, *siccar*, sure, certain, safe (cf. German *sicher*).

Skep, a straw basket, straw beehive.

Skeyte, to bounce.

Skime, a glance of reflected light, variant of *shimmer*.

Skirl, to scream; a shrill piercing sound.

Slee, sly, cunning.

Slipmalabours, an idle, unreliable person.

Smee, smooth.

Smoor, to smother.

Sock, a ploughshare.

Sonsie, *sonsy*, wholesome; *unsonsie*, evil or ill-boding.

Sook, to suck, suckle.

Sowens, the dust of oatmeal steeped and cooked, the food of the very poor. "The goodwife threw some dust into a pot of water and by the grace of God it turned into a pudding." On the other hand, when carefully made, it was considered a delicacy for invalids. A Galloway woman left the recipe: "The husks were steeped in water for some days, then a sieve separated them from the meal and water. Fresh water was added, the mixture stirred and allowed to stand till it soured. After fully a week it was boiled, with constant and careful stirring. When poured into basins (called goans) it would be as smooth and firm as butter, something like thick cornflour, tasting neither sour nor sweet, and much appreciated" (Richard Tarbet, *Old Buittle*).

Speer, *speir*, to ask.

Spelder, to split, pull apart, spread out.

Spotch, *spouse*, to search or seek; variant of poach.

Sprit-binnings, hay ropes; *sprit hay*, bog hay. (*Sprit*, a coarse rush growing in marshy ground often used for rope-making and thatching.)

Spurtle, a wooden implement for (i) baking; (ii) stirring porridge (cf. *spatula*).

Steek, to push shut, stick.

Stoond, a blow (cf. stun, astound).

Stour, dust (in a state of motion); cognate with stir.

Studdy, a blacksmith's anvil (in archaic Engl., *stithy*).

Swarf, *swerf*, to faint.

Swee, an iron hook for hanging a pot or kettle over the fire; a swing.

Sweir, reluctant, unwilling.

Syne, then; *sinsyne*, since.

Taid, a toad.

Taigle, to hinder, tarry.

Tane and tither, the one and the other.

Tent, guard, care; *tak' tent till*, to take care of, watch over.

Thack, thatch.

Thir, these (of objects near at hand).

Thrang, very busy; cognate with throng(ed).

Thrawn, twisted, cross-grained; *thrawn weather* is cold and disagreeable.

Threep, urge, assert; *to keep one's threep*, to hold one's counsel. Lady Ashton *kept her threep*.

Thristle, a thistle.

Thrums, the bunch of threads constituting the end of the web. (J. M. Barrie used this word as a literary pseudonym for his native Kirriemuir.)

Timersome, easily frightened.

Tine, *tyne*, to lose; *tint*, lost.

Tiravee, a fit of temper.

Tirl, the same as dirl (q.v.) in *Aiken Drum*, it means to tarry. A *tirling-pin* was a kind of door knocker used in bygone days. A metal ring was hung over a threaded pin, and when moved up and down produced a loud vibration. This was known as *tirling the pin*; and Aiken Drum *tirled na lang*, i.e. gave a perfunctory announcement of his presence before entering the gate of the township.

Tod Lowrie, a fox. Lowrie/Laurie is the name for a fox in Scotland as Reynard is in England.

Toom, empty; *toom-skinned*, hungry; *toom-heided*, stupid; *to come back toom-tailed*, object not attained; *toom-tabard*, Empty Coat, the name for John Balliol.

Tow, hemp, thread; *have other tow on the rock*, have other fish to fry; *tow-rock*, spindle thread.

Tyke, a dog, usually of low degree.

Ugsome, awesome, fearful.

Vaguing, wandering; *vague*, to wander (cf. Latin *vagare*).

Wab, a web; *wabster*, a weaver.

Wale, to choose (cf. German *Wahl*, choice). *Waly* or *wally* originally meant choice or beautiful (cf. Tam o' Shanter's *winsome wench and waly*); then it came to mean ornamental—*wally dugs* are the porcelain dogs which were found at Scottish firesides at the turn of the century. Later still the word came to be used exclusively for porcelain, so that false teeth in common Scottish parlance are *wally-teeth* and the tiled passageways of tenement houses are known as *wally-closes*.

Wallidreg, a weakling. The youngest bird in the nest; "the shakings o' the poke".

Want, to need, be without; *wantin' the breeks*, trouserless.

Wear, to separate.

Warsal, *warsle*, *warstle*, to wrestle, to struggle through.

Wauchie, pale, sallow, as applied to skin.

Waughorn, the devil.

Waur, worse.

Wean, a child (contraction of *wee ane*); *weanling*, infant.

Wearifu', oppressive.

Weel-faured, handsome, well-favoured.

Weird, to prophesy; as a noun, fate. *Dree your weird*, suffer your fate.

Wheen, a number; *a gey wheen*, a good number.

Whinge, to whine.

Whink, the suppressed, excited bark of a sheep dog on the alert.
Whomel, *whummle*, to turn upside down, overcome, submerge.
Wile, see *wale*.
Win, or *wun oot*, to escape.
Winnock-sole, window ledge.
Wolron, a feeble creature.
Won, to dwell; *wonner*, an inhabitant (cf. German *wohnen*, to dwell).
Wyte, to blame.

Yammer, to fret, whine, cry (cf. German *Jammer*, grief).
Yell, *yeld*, *eild*, a cow not giving milk; *a yell field*, a barren field; *a yell rock*, one that won't quarry without gunpowder.
Yerk, to beat, strike, bind tightly; *a yerkit coat*, one that is too tight.
Yill, ale; *yill-cap een*, eyes like saucers.
Yird, to bury (lit. to earth); *yirth*, earth; *unyirthly*, unearthly.
Yowl, howl.

BIBLIOGRAPHY

Aarne, Antti, *Types of Folklore* Helsinki 1964
Aberdeen Breviary 1509
Aelred of Rievaux, *The Life of St. Ninian* (The Historians of Scotland, Vol. 5) Edinburgh 1874
Aytoun, W. E., *Ballads of Scotland* Edinburgh 1858
Bergen, F. D., *American Folklore Society Journal*, Vol. 3
Berwickshire Naturalists' Club, Transactions, Vol. xxiii
Brown, J. Wood, *The Life and Legend of Michael Scot* Edinburgh 1879
Buchan, John, *Sir Walter Scott* London 1932
Buchan, Peter, "Ancient Scottish Tales from the Recitations of the Aged Sybils in the North Countrie" MS, privately printed 1908 Peterhead
Campbell, Lord Archibald, *Waifs and Strays of Celtic Tradition I* London 1889
Campbell, J. F., *Popular Tales of the West Highlands* Glasgow 1860
Carlyle, Thomas, *Reminiscences* London 1887
The Castle Douglas Miscellany, Vol. 2, 1825
Chadwick, N. H., *Studies in the Early British Church* Cambridge 1958
Chambers, Robert, *Popular Rhymes of Scotland* Edinburgh 1826
Child, F. J., *English and Scottish Popular Ballads* Boston 1882-98
Clodd, Edward, *Tom Tit Tot* London 1898
The Complaynt of Scotland, c. 1548
Cox, M. R., *Cinderella* London 1893
County Folklore: Clackmannan, Fife, Northern Counties and Borders, Orkney and Shetland
Cromek, R. H., *Remains of Galloway and Nithsdale Song* London 1810
"Dee" (Dunn, M. T.), "Ghaisties and Ferlies" *Gallovidian Annual* No. xiii, 1932
"A Tale of St. Ringan" *Gallovidian Annual* No. xiv, 1933
Douglas, Sir George, *Scottish Fairy and Folk Tales* London 1892
Dumfries and Galloway Naturalist and Antiquarian Society, Transactions
Edinburgh Annual Register 1811. "Biographical Memoir of Dr Leyden"
Fairweather, Barbara, *Folklore of Glencoe and North Lorn*. Published by the Glencoe and North Lorn Folk Museum, 1971
The Folklore Journal, Vols. I, II, IV, VII, 1878-89
The Folklore Record, Vol. I, 1878
Folio B 643041 Mitchell Library. (Article on Glasgow's Arms.)
Fortnightly Review 1873 Vol. xiii
Galt, John, *Annals of the Parish* Edinburgh 1881
Grimm, Brothers, *Household Tales* London 1884
Hawick Archaeological Society, Transactions 69-75
Harper, M. M., *Rambles in Galloway* Edinburgh 1876
Henderson, William, *Notes on the Folklore of the Northern Counties and the Borders* London 1866

Hogg, David, *Life of Allan Cunningham* Dumfries 1866
Hogg, James, *The Queen's Wake* Edinburgh 1813 *Poetical Works*
Jackson, K. H., *The International Popular Tale and the Early Welsh Tradition* Cardiff 1961
  "Sources for the Life of St Kentigern", see Chadwick, *Studies in the Early British Church*)
Kirk, Robert, *Secret Commonwealth of Elves, Fauns and Fairies* (1691) Edinburgh 1815
Leyden, John, *Scenes of Infancy* Edinburgh 1803
Lyndsay of the Mount, Sir David, *Armorial*, 1542. Folio 1822, National Library of Scotland
Mackenzie, Donald, Article on the Arms of Glasgow, B 643041, Mitchell Library
Mactaggart, John, *The Gallovidian Encyclopedia* London 1824
Miller, Hugh, *The Old Red Sandstone* Edinburgh 1847
Motherwell, William, *Minstrelsy Ancient and Modern* London 1827
Nicholson, William, *Tales in Verse and Miscellaneous Poems* Edinburgh 1814
Puttenham, George, *The Arte of English Poesie* London 1589
Recollections of a Roxburghshire Woman, privately printed. Craig-Brown Collection, Selkirk Public Library
Reid, R. C., "Traditions of Kirkcowan", MSS Ewart Library, Dumfries
Robertson, W., *Historical Tales of Ayrshire* Glasgow 1889
Russell, James, *Reminiscences of Yarrow* Edinburgh 1886
Scott, Sir Walter, *Minstrelsy of the Scottish Border* Edinburgh 1802
  Lady of the Lake (Notes) Edinburgh 1810
  Lay of the Last Minstrel (Notes) Edinburgh 1805
  Letters on Demonology and Witchcraft Edinburgh 1830
  Redgauntlet Edinburgh 1824
Scottish Notes and Queries, Vol. iv, No. 3, 1890
Simpson, Robert, *The Cottars of the Glen: A Glimpse of Rural Life a Hundred Years Agone* Glasgow 1866
Spence, Lewis, *The Fairy Tradition in Britain* London 1848
Stevenson, William, *Legends of St Kentigern* Edinburgh 1847
Tarbet, Richard, *Old Bittle* London
Thompson, Stith, *The Types of the Folktale* London 1964
Tolkien, J. R. R., *Tree and Leaf* London 1964
Train, Joseph, "Letters etc." Unpublished MS 874, National Library of Scotland
Trotter, R. De B.,"Galloway Superstitions" *Gallovidian Annual*, Vol. 5, 1903
Veitch, John, *History and Poetry of the Scottish Border* Glasgow 1878
Warrack, John, *Domestic Life in Scotland 1488-1688* London 1920
Wilkie, Thomas, "Old Rites, Customs and Ceremonies of the Inhabitants of the Southern Counties of Scotland", MS 121, National Library of Scotland. (See also Transactions of Berwickshire Naturalists' Club, Vol. xxiii)
Wood, J. Maxwell, "Superstitious Record in the South-West of Scotland" *Gallovidian Annual*, No. xi, 1909